Hen
Pecked

A Salt Mine Novel

Joseph Browning   Suzi Yee

Text Copyright © 2020 by Joseph Browning and Suzi Yee

Published by Expeditious Retreat Press
Cover by J Caleb Design
Edited by Elizabeth VanZwoll

For information regarding Joseph Browning and Suzi Yee's novels and to subscribe to their mailing list, see their website at https://www.joseph-browning.com

To follow them on Twitter: https://twitter.com/Joseph_Browning

To follow Joseph on Facebook: https://www.facebook.com/joseph.browning.52

To follow Suzi on Facebook: https://www.facebook.com/SuziYeeAuthor/

To follow them on MeWe: https://mewe.com/i/josephbrowning

By Joseph Browning and Suzi Yee

The Salt Mine Novels

Money Hungry
Feeding Frenzy
Ground Rules
Mirror Mirror
Bottom Line
Whip Smart

Rest Assured
Hen Pecked
Brain Drain
Bone Dry
Vicious Circle
High Horse

Chapter One

McMillian, Michigan, USA
15th of November, 10:40 p.m. (GMT-5)

The high beams of Carl Dalton's Ford F150 lit the wide width of the dark two-lane county road, pushing against the woods that loomed over the crumbly asphalt. The engine comfortably growled as he drove deeper into the woods toward the hunting cabin that had been in his family for decades. In the age of glamping and country homes, the Dalton hunting lodge remained honest to its rustic roots. If you were cold, there was a fireplace and cords of dried wood. If you needed water, there was a well. If you needed a bath, there was a small lake. If you needed supplies, it was a short drive to McMillian, and the deer processor was in nearby Newberry. It was the perfect place to escape for a week under the guise of hunting; even if you were to invite your wife and kids for some reason, they wouldn't want to come.

He led the caravan of three vehicles onto a gravel road that dead-ended on his acreage and pulled to the side of the cabin, leaving enough space for the two SUVs that followed him. It was a small group this year, but Carl didn't mind. They were all experienced hunters, and none of them got on his nerves much, which was better than the year his wife had insisted on him bringing his dumbass son-in-law "so they could bond." His new orange camos and shiny, pristine gun were the least of his offenses that weekend—man couldn't go five minutes without talking, and kept checking his phone even after he was told that the coverage was spotty at best.

Dave, Pete, and Joe got out of their vehicles and stretched their legs. It was a five-hour drive with traffic, but it was worth it to be out here where the stars shined brighter and there wasn't a neighbor for miles. Carl unlocked the cabin, and they started unloading their gear. He'd come out last month to get everything ready for hunting season, so there was minimal fumbling as he lit the lantern and made his way to the fireplace. He stacked the logs and lit a fire starter, coaxing the embers until the flame took.

Once everything was inside and they had called cots, they started their ten-day hunting trip as they always did: steaks, cigars, and beer. Joe opened up the cooler and pulled out his church key, handing each man a bottle. They'd made it up to the cabin for another hunt, which was as good a reason to celebrate as any. Summer was for family vacations and the holidays were for the women in their lives. They just had to show up, dress appropriately, and play their part. But hunting season? That was their time. It was their reward for surviving Disney World and agreeing to visit the in-laws at Christmas.

Dave was the cook among them, and he pulled the seasoned cast iron skillet off its hook on the wall. He unwrapped the beautifully marbled ribeyes from the butcher paper and sprinkled a little salt and pepper on each side—that was all a good piece of beef needed. He waited until the pan was hot before throwing the first slab on. The smell and sizzle made their mouths water.

"Do you know how long it's been since I've had a steak?!" Pete griped. "Debbie's got it into her head that we should be eating vegetarian, except somehow fish and chicken don't count as meat."

"Strange vegetable, the chicken." Carl cracked. "You should get her on that Atkin's diet—never ate so many pork chops, steaks, and bacon on a regular basis until Julie saw what it did to our cholesterol."

"Is that the gluten-free one?" Joe asked. "I thought I heard wrong when Jenny told me we were no longer eating bread because gluten is unhealthy. Isn't bread the whole reason civilization developed?" he said indignantly. "And whoever heard of using lettuce as a hamburger bun?"

"No, Atkin's cuts out all carbs; no fruit, milk, pasta, rice, potatoes, beans, carrots, peas—nada," Dave answered. "And it was beer that created civilization," he added, raising his bottle.

"What the hell's left to eat?" Joe puzzled.

"Meat and non-starchy vegetables," Dave said as he turned the steak over and approved of the char—he was strictly a one-flip man. "They *do* sell gluten-free bread and crackers at the store now."

Joe scoffed. "No thanks. Those taste worse than not having it at all."

"Hey, you guys in for ice fishing?" Pete chimed in. "I may be able to get my father-in-law's place if we can figure out a time."

"Maybe sometime in January? After the holidays and the kids are back in school," Joe suggested.

"I'm out for January," Carl replied. "Laney is due then, and we're going out to California after New Year's to help."

Dave gave him a look of disbelief. "What are you going to do in California for a month?"

Carl shrugged. "Put together a crib or paint the baby room—whatever Julie and Laney want me to do. Probably scare the living shit out of my son-in-law, who has no idea how much his life is about to change," he posited and took a swig of his beer with a thick smile. His companions all grinned and nodded knowingly. "Maybe try avocado toast and see what all the fuss is about."

"That's a long time to spend on the Left Coast—don't come back all liberal on us," Joe joked.

Dave laughed at the notion and squeezed the meat with his tongs—just the right give for medium rare. "First steak's ready. Eat up while I get the next one cooking."

They spent the next hour eating, drinking, and smoking

before calling it a night. They would start early tomorrow, setting up their blinds just before daybreak and positioning themselves for hours of waiting. In this part of the Upper Peninsula, there was no antlerless hunting permitted and a three-point antler restriction, not that Carl would have reported any of his hunting buddies for a slip up, but Pete was a real stickler for the rules. Last weekend, he almost caused a ruckus when someone wanted to put out a salt lick, citing the ban on bait in the Lower Peninsula to reduce the spread of chronic wasting disease.

More counties reported cases each year, and deer check stations popped up all over during hunting season so the heads could be tested for it. Last year, he bagged a beautiful four-point buck in the Lower Peninsula and had to wait for it to be cleared before he could have it mounted. Deer shot in Luce County weren't required to be tested for chronic wasting disease, but there was a deer check station in Newberry. It didn't cost anything, and Carl didn't like to take chances. Officially, the Department of Natural Resources said there wasn't any evidence that it was transmittable to humans, but they still recommended people avoid eating meat from CWD-positive animals. That's all he needed—the deer version of mad cow disease.

Between the long drive, the food, the beer, and the peace and quiet, sleep came easy. Not even Joe's snoring kept them up—can't run a C-pap machine without electricity. It was still dark when they exited the cabin in the morning with jerky-stuffed pockets and a thermos of coffee, thick and black enough to repave the roads. They were familiar with the lay of the land and had their sights on prime real estate: a clearing by a stream where deer were known to drink and graze. As they neared, a streak of orange on the ground caught Pete's eye.

"Anyone here?" he called out in case another hunter had claimed their first choice for a blind. The woods were quiet, and the men approached, rifles down.

The smell hit them first: they had killed enough animals to know the odor of death from meat that had gone off. Dave was the first to see them, and he recoiled at the sight—there were two dressed in hunter's orange lying face up, bodies torn and half-eaten. Their empty eye sockets glared up at him, and their mouths were agape. Their guns lay beside them, one of them a shiny AR-15. Pete didn't like to think ill of the dead, but he reckoned any hunter that needed that many bullets to hit a deer wasn't much of a shot.

Carl took off his hat and slapped it against his thigh. "Shit," he cursed. The scavengers had made a mess of things, and they were technically on his property. He knew he didn't have anything to do with it—there were no buried traps or anything—but he suspected he was going to get dragged into it one way or another. He took a long breath and composed himself, running his hand through his short gray hair before putting his hat back on. He slung his rifle back on his arm and said plainly, "I'll go get some help."

Chapter Two

Detroit, Michigan, USA
19th of November, 6:05 a.m. (GMT-5)

Teresa Martinez could see her breath in the cold morning air as her steps rhythmically beat against the pavement. Her short ponytail swung opposite her hips as she strode in time with the music streaming in through her ear buds. Running was a form of meditation for Martinez, something she did when she needed to think, clear her mind, or just be. She loved the crisp weather and crunch of fallen leaves underfoot and had taken to running in the morning instead of after work once daylight savings had ended—fewer cars and joggers alike. If she kept this up until Thanksgiving, she would actually be sleeping in the day of the race.

She rounded the corner and headed back to her Corktown residence—a two-story house with a grill in the backyard and a covered porch in the front that she rented from Wilson, the Salt Mine agent that had trained her. It was warded out the wazoo and came with its own ritual room behind a secret door in the basement. It also came with roommates: the ghosts of three Quakers whose claim to this plot of land predated Wilson's or hers. Thankfully, Mille, Wolfhard, and the quiet one all seemed to like her, and they peaceably shared the house. Her guest bedroom was currently occupied by Stigma, another Salt Mine agent, who'd needed a place to recuperate and be reborn as Aaron Haddock, Discretion Minerals's newest engineer. The house in Corktown was slowly becoming home, and its only real drawback was that it didn't have a dishwasher.

Martinez noted her time as she hit the porch—five miles in forty-three minutes. It wasn't a bad time, but she was hoping to finish the 10K in fifty and would have to pick up the pace. She had a little over a week to train and get her running partner up to speed. Martinez was well into her cooldown and stretches on the living room floor when Haddock, breathless, came through the front door. He held himself up with his hands on his thighs and leaned against the front door for support.

"You're trying to kill me," he said resolutely.

"You're the one that asked me to help you get back into shape," she reminded him as she pulled out her foam roller and hit her long lean quads and IT band.

"It's only fair since you fattened me up," he pointed out.

"I didn't hold the fork to your mouth," she said sharply.

Haddock cut his eyes at her and raised his register. "'Let's do the Turkey Trot this year,' she said. 'It will be fun,' she said. 'The 5K is hardly a challenge, let's sign up for the 10K,'" he parroted her as he stretched his calves and hamstrings against the back of the couch. They ached at the suggestion.

Martinez laughed. "You were the one that talked me into swept away bangs—consider this payback," she said evenly.

"I stand by that call—they really framed and softened your face," he said emphatically.

"You can't tell me my routine is worse than what the Russian Navy put you through," she said sardonically and ran up the stairs to hit the shower first. The water heater was generally good for two showers, but this was the only way to be sure hers was steaming.

"Relentless!" he yelled at her before collapsing on the ground supine, telling himself he was doing yoga. He heard the plumbing rumble as Martinez turned on the water for her shower—which would last fifteen minutes, plus or minus two minutes. It wasn't that she was anal retentive or compulsive about it, just that she was consistent. It was exactly what he needed when he came out of deep cover, busted up and brooding over the mistakes of multiple aliases. During the past three months, he had come to learn her routine and preferences, mostly in an attempt to disrupt her life as little as possible, but he hadn't expected to have so much fun. They destressed with good food and bad TV, danced to loud music while they cooked and baked, and gave each other plenty of space and privacy in between.

Their cohabitation was soon coming to an end, as Haddock built something that resembled a normal life—a cover for his real work at the Salt Mine. He was closing on his new place in a few weeks, and nothing says "unassuming citizen" like a W-2 job and a mortgage. It was a nice loft in a converted warehouse with an open floor plan and lots of potential. He could start from scratch, decorating and sculpting the space as he made similar decisions about who exactly Aaron Haddock was going to be.

Officially, he was on half-duty and getting a refresher from the librarians, with whom he'd had no contact for five years while he was in deep cover in Ivory Tower turf. Once he was cleared for full duty, he wasn't expecting to spend much time in Detroit and just needed a place that was his own. He didn't need a lot of space, since he always carried important things on his person as tattoos. When he was first recruited, the librarians called him a scribe, a magician who could impart magic into ink. He didn't know it had a name, only that he knew how to turn physical objects into tattoos on his skin that could be retrieved at a later time. He liked to change things around so no one could identify him by his ink, but those that really knew him knew what to look for…not that many people knew him that well.

When he heard the water cut out, he realized how long he had been lying on the floor and made an honest attempt at doing some push-ups and sit-ups to cover his prolonged dead man's pose before heading to take his own shower in the guest bathroom. By the time he was back downstairs, Martinez was already dressed and ready for work. Her oversized leather tote bag was on the hall table, and she had already brewed coffee, made omelets for breakfast, and packed her lunch. Haddock grinned to himself—dependable, like clockwork.

Martinez had a pensive look on her face when he took a seat at the table opposite her. "Penny for your thoughts?" he asked after his first sip of hot coffee.

"Thanksgiving," she said between bites. "How would you feel about a traditional dinner?"

"Like turkey, mashed potatoes, green bean casserole, and pumpkin pie?" he said quizzically. "That's a lot of food for two people."

"Well, I was thinking of opening it up and inviting anyone from work that didn't have somewhere else to be for the holidays, assuming they're not out on assignment," she replied a little too casually.

"You've been plotting this for a while, haven't you?" he voiced his suspicion.

"I just think it would be nice to give people who don't have a family somewhere to go on a holiday that's all about family," she reasoned.

He chewed a few more times before swallowing and chose his words wisely. "Don't think it would be counterproductive for all of us to be in one place, you know, since we are all secret agents for a black ops organization?"

"Well, we're also all employees of Discretion Minerals," she rebutted. "But I see your point. What if we kept it small—just

Wilson and LaSalle? Wilson owns the house, and LaSalle has already stopped by a few times. I could do a duck or goose instead of a turkey. Or maybe a Cornish hen for each of us," she spouted options off the top of her head.

"Frankly, the choice of poultry isn't my biggest concern," he said lightly and leaned forward, resting his head on his hand. "So you want to wake up before sunrise, run a 10K, attend the parade downtown, and then cook a full meal and entertain," he enumerated what her theoretical Thanksgiving day would look like.

She shrugged with aplomb. "Assuming duty doesn't call… yeah. Sounds like fun, like Thanksgiving for misfits."

He rolled his eyes and threw his hands up. "I'm in. But if you get called away for work, the party's off. No way I'm hosting a Thanksgiving dinner by myself."

"Deal," she agreed with a self-satisfied smile. She didn't need his permission to host a Thanksgiving meal at her own house, but it was more fun this way. She glanced at the clock on the wall and jumped to her feet. "I've got to get going." She grabbed her travel mug of coffee and picked up her bag on her way out the door. "Later."

"Later," he replied to the closed door and poured himself a second cup.

Martinez slid into her black Hellcat, which looked conspicuously out of place next to the cool-gray khaki Subaru Crosstrek sitting in her driveway. Apparently, Aaron Haddock was all about affordable but elegant engineering. Either that or he was a lesbian in need of a kayak and two big dogs. The engine purred on ignition, and she drove toward Zug Island.

There was a buzz in the air, and Martinez knew things were in motion. Soon, she would have the house to herself again, Wilson would be back to work, and she would be nearing completion of her first year at the Salt Mine. There wasn't a greeting card for it, but she felt she should do something to mark the occasion—maybe take Moncrief up on her offer of a girl's weekend in the Greek Isles once Wilson and Haddock were back to work.

Eleven months in, she still wasn't exactly sure why she was recruited to the Salt Mine. Through inference, she'd pieced together some of the other agent's specialties, but she still wasn't sure what hers was. She had seen the unbelievable, uncovered the most slippery of plots, and was the first known person to bring something back from the Magh Meall without facing any of the normal consequences. It wasn't exactly the kind of thing she could put under "special skills" on her resume, but she figured it had to count for something.

She stopped at the gate and presented the ID badge bearing her likeness with the name Tessa Marvel, Assistant Director of Acquisitions for Discretion Minerals. The guard raised the barrier and waved her through, and she pulled into the underground parking lot. She mechanically inserted her titanium keys, presented her palm and retina for scanning, and made her way past Abrams—who was still blonde and onto a new beau—to her fifth-floor office buried deep in the mines. All this seemed so cloak and dagger when she first interviewed, and now it was routine—just another workday ferreting, hunting down, and neutralizing supernatural threats.

She put away her things and skimmed her in-basket while her computer booted up. There was the ubiquitous manila folder labeled OFFICIAL – SM EYES ONLY in black ink that was colloquially called the dailies—a topical briefing culled from the CIA and FBI as it intersected with their concerns. When she grabbed it from the top of the stack, she saw beneath it bright red lettering on a green folder: AGENT RESTRICTED – SM EYES ONLY. She put the dailies aside and opened the dossier containing the details required for her upcoming assignment and impending visit to the fourth floor.

The bulk of the file was dedicated to the Keweenaw Bay Indian Community of the historic Lake Superior Band of Chippewa Indians, or the Ojibwa Anishinabek, as they referred to themselves in their original language. There was a sizable population in Michigan's Upper Peninsula and various plots of land were designated as their permanent homeland, including the L'Anse Indian Reservation and Bay Mills Indian Community. The Salt Mine, under the guise of the Institute of Tradition, worked closely with the indigenous population to their mutual benefit. The tribes were infused with support and funds to preserve, practice, and pass on their traditions, and the

Mine gained intimate knowledge of another magical discipline native to North America that spanned the Western Great Lakes region, including parts of Michigan, Wisconsin, Minnesota, North Dakota, Ontario, and Manitoba.

Martinez flipped through the raw demographic and cultural information and got to the interesting part: their magic. The librarians did their best to identify the actual magic from the extraneous cultural customs that came with every religion or belief system. It was a task made extremely difficult by the fact that many indigenous people passed their knowledge in an oral tradition, and the Ojibwe language—one of many that belonged to the Algonquian language family—was rarely spoken outside of the community, if at all.

While every tribe had their own unique beliefs and practices, there were certain similarities that were shared across the various groups in the Lake Superior Band of Chippewa Indians: a quadripartite belief system, a strong affinity for nature, the seven grandfather teachings, and manitous, also known as manidoo or manidoowag depending on the tribe.

Manitous were spirits or gods that powered life, both as an omnipresent force symbolized by animal spirits as well as a more monotheistic idea of Gichi Manidoo—the Great Spirit. In Ojibwa tribes, shamans and healers could access them and their power through specialized ritual knowledge which had only been written down in recent history.

As far as the Salt Mine classification, manitous were a

type of supernatural creature that resided in the Magh Meall of North America. They weren't inherently good nor evil, and therefore subject to the full range of motivations. One of the more popular programs funded by the Institute of Tradition was the regular performance of rituals to encourage the helpful manitous and ward off the malevolent ones. The tribes retained all control on the execution and presentation of the rituals, and the Keweenaw Bay Indian Community was willing to partner with people who respected their commitment to self-determination and decolonization.

At the end, Martinez found an ID and background for Tracy Martin, her alias as a correspondent for the Institute of Tradition. There was information on their contact at the L'Anse Reservation, the oldest and largest permanent homeland for the Chippewa in Michigan, created under the Chippewa Treaty of 1854. Martinez understood why she was chosen for the mission, even though there were more experienced agents in town—Latinos have the largest percentage crossover of Native American heritage, and she looked the part.

Martinez picked up her coffee and started reading in earnest. She was somewhere in the four sacred medicines—apparently, not all sage smudges were phooey—when the intercom box affixed to the corner of her desk blinked red and buzzed. She pressed the button and answered perfunctorily, "This is Lancer."

"Good morning, Lancer," David LaSalle's precise tenor came out of the comm. "Leader would like to see you this morning—9:15 if possible."

A summons from Leader was not an invitation, it was an order, but she appreciated the illusion of choice he offered. A mischievous smile spread across her face as she contemplated answering, "No, that doesn't work for me; how about 11:00?" The brief conniption that would follow was tempting, but hardly an appropriate way to repay his politeness.

Martinez put her playful flights of fancy aside and replied, "Sure, I'll be there at 9:15." The connection cut out when she released the button, and she returned to her reading, checking her watch every so often.

Chapter Three

Detroit, Michigan, USA
19th of November, 9:13 a.m. (GMT-5)

"Lancer is here for your 9:15," LaSalle announced to the petite salt-and-pepper-haired woman sitting behind the large desk. A bank of filing cabinets lined the wall behind her, and the clean white walls carved out of salt gleamed in the lighting.

"Thank you, David," Leader curtly dismissed him and motioned for Martinez to enter while she rose to her full five feet to pull the correct file. Leader was a slim woman somewhere past sixty, dressed in jeans and a cardigan draped over a scoop-necked t-shirt. Her casual clothing and simple bob did little to mask her intensity and indomitable will. When Leader turned her hawkish gray eyes on you, everything else fell away.

Martinez complied, brushing past LaSalle, and took a seat in one of the oversized chairs. Her legs were long enough to sit all the way back and still have her feet firmly flat on the ground. She filled the excess lateral space with her leather bag and extracted the green folder that had been in her in basket and a legal pad for taking notes. She wouldn't go so far as to say she was used to Leader, but she was learning how to offset some of the discomfort. Leader returned to her seat, file in hand. Martinez let her gaze fall on a spot on the wall behind Leader and made that her visual anchor. It gave her the appearance of looking at Leader without actually making direct eye contact.

"This weekend, a pair of hunters were found dead in the eastern Upper Peninsula, bodies badly mauled. This is the third incident since the start of deer hunting season in October. There are always some hunting fatalities, but these fall outside of normal parameters." Leader started and laid out pictures facing Martinez. "As you can see, they're a mess. There was no evidence of self-inflicted or accidental firearm discharge, nor was there any evidence of a defensive attack by an injured deer. There are no grizzlies in the UP, but there are black bear, wolves, and cougars.

"As you can see, the first two were lone hunters, but the latest was a pair of hunters equipped with firearms even though it was technically bow hunting season. Their weapons hadn't been discharged and the lack of defensive fire suggests these are not animal attacks. Something attacked them before either could get a shot off. Your mission is to determine if that something is supernatural in nature. If you are facing an aggressive manitou, further intervention will be necessary, but it may be handled by the locals according to their custom, with some appropriate guidance," Leader euphemized.

"You have the GPS coordinates to all three sites and a list of common manitou signatures. There will be more activity in the area due to hunting season and the last site is on private property, so if you have to pull out your FBI ID to gain access, so be it. Be sure to bring hunter orange. We have arranged accommodations at the Ojibwa Casino in Baraga," Leader concluded. She put everything back in place and slid the folder across the table. Leader looked up and caught Martinez's brown eyes before she could employ her trick. "Do you have any questions?"

"No, it seems pretty straightforward," Martinez responded plainly and broke eye contact to retrieve the folder and put it in her bag with the rest of her things.

"Good. Visit Weber before you leave town for appropriate gear," she dismissed Lancer and shuffled to the next file on her desk. "I'm sure David can help you get down there."

Martinez paused a millisecond but found no chink in her stony facade. She rose from the chair and left with a deferential, "Yes, Leader." She closed the door behind her and breathed easy once there was more space and solid slab of wood between her and Leader. LaSalle was typing away at his desk; his long fingers covered the keyboard with ease. He was typing up the handwritten document that sat to one side of his screen but looked up when she hadn't moved from her spot after a few seconds.

"Everything okay?" he asked.

"Yeah. Just getting my bearings," Martinez replied. "Can you get me to the sixth floor? I've got a German to visit," she quipped.

"Of course, just give me a second," he said with a nod as he closed and secured the document and his computer. LaSalle rose and escorted her to the elevators. Martinez liked that he was tall. At five-foot-ten, there weren't many men with whom she could wear heels without towering over them. As they waited side-by-side, they made casual conversation, sticking to benign topics that were safe for two colleagues, like the weather or how Christmas needed to back off and let Thanksgiving have its time.

After the elevator arrived, she piped up, "Speaking of Thanksgiving, Aaron and I are thinking of having a traditional dinner. You're more than welcome to join us, if you don't already have plans and I'm not chasing down monsters," she qualified.

He smirked and looked down at her. "That sounds nice but that's only a week away. Don't you think you're tempting fate by making plans, especially with a new assignment?" The doors opened and they stepped inside. He held his palm and retina to the scanners.

"I don't think of them as plans as much as scheduled serendipity," she explained. "I'll even let you bring something if you want."

"I do make a mean sweet potato pie," he warned as he pressed the button for level six and stepped out of the elevator.

"Then it's a definite maybe?" she asked.

"Why not?" he said with a shrug and a smile as the door closed.

Martinez suppressed her glee on the ride two floors down and regained her composure by the time she stepped onto the sixth floor. She wound her way through the hallways cut from the salt and took the turn that led her to the domain of Harold Weber, Salt Mine's quartermaster and inventor extraordinaire.

She heard him muttering to himself before she saw him. She stood outside his open door and knocked to alert him of her presence before entering. He ruffled his unruly white hair as he pulled up his safety goggles on top of his head and flashed his bright blues eyes at her.

"Ah, Lancer, you're here. Come in, come in," he welcomed and cleared a seat for her. "I'll just be a minute," he warned her as he dropped his glasses back down and made the final adjustment to his current project. Every surface was covered with paperwork, tools, or bits of inventions that hadn't yet found their final forms, but Martinez knew better than to touch anything. Weber had a system, and she waited for him to finish what he was doing before getting to her gear.

Weber took the mechanism in hand and flicked the switch back and forth, watching the spark it made when it completed its magical circuit. "*Wunderbar!*" he exclaimed and put it off to one side. He set the goggles down beside it and wiped his hands with the clean rag from one of the many pockets of his work apron. "Now, let's see what we have for you today," he spoke deliberately as he straightened his thick prescription lenses. "Ah, yes, you're heading into the Indian territory."

"I think they prefer to be called indigenous people or Native Americans," she gently corrected him.

He tilted his head to concede to her point and proceeded. "Your general North American banishment bullets should cover everything, but here's a box of specialized ammunition that has better coverage for Amerindian supernatural creatures." He noted Martinez's smile as approval for his vocabulary change but didn't draw attention to it. "Should you require the assistance of a local magician who practices the traditional way, you'll need this."

Martinez opened the satchel he handed her, and a rich almost sweet aroma spilled out. "What is it?"

"Asema, or traditional tobacco…more precisely, Nicotiana rustica, with roasted red willow tree bark, sage, sweet grass, and cedar. It's got all four medicines packed in there and will make a nice offering for any ritual," he answered in full and sternly added, "Make sure you read the etiquette Chloe and Dot gave you on visiting a shaman." Martinez gave him a hard stare; of course she'd read the etiquette guide. Who did he think she was—Hobgoblin?

"I also have these," Weber said, handing her a box. "When you wear them, it will soften your step and help you sneak around if you find yourself stalking prey on your trip."

Intrigued, Martinez pulled back the acid-free paper to

reveal a pair of moccasins. The leather was soft and supple to the touch, and she recognized a few of the symbols decorating the slippers. The only problem was that they were about the length of her palm. "Will they work if I wear them on my hands?" she asked pertly.

"They'll fit. It's magic," he reassured her, "but you're more than welcome to try them on here if you're skeptical."

Martinez had seen magical rings self-size—why not shoes? "No, I trust you," she said as she put the moccasins back in their box. "Random question…what are you doing for Thanksgiving?"

He shrugged. "It's just another day for me. They usually have turkey and stuffing sandwiches with cranberry relish in the commissary for the people working that day." Unlike other businesses, the Salt Mine never closed.

"How would you like a home-cooked meal and convivial company this year? That is, assuming I don't get mauled in the woods of the Upper Peninsula and the world doesn't end in the next week," she joked darkly. "It's my first Thanksgiving in Detroit and I'm a little short on family."

"Who's coming?" he inquired; he didn't particularly care for chitchat with strangers.

"It's sort of a new development, so the guest list is in flux. Stigma, myself, maybe LaSalle and Fulcrum. I haven't spoken to the twins yet, but they would be welcome if they don't have plans. Basically an open invitation for Salt Mine agents that will be in town and don't have other engagements."

He raised an eyebrow. "Have you asked Leader?"

"Not yet," she admitted. "I kinda wanted to field interest before I brought it to her attention. Do you think she'd want to come?"

Weber shook his head equivocally. "Maybe, maybe not, but who doesn't want to be invited?" he asked rhetorically.

Chapter Four

Baraga, Michigan, USA
19th of November, 8:00 p.m. (GMT-5)

Martinez pulled her rented Jeep Cherokee Trailhawk into the parking lot of the Ojibwa Casino Hotel Baraga. The neon letters and emblematic soaring eagle lit up the night, and the exterior lights tucked behind overhangs and ground cover formed a row of stacked triangles along the face of the long building. Owned and operated by the Keweenaw Bay Indian Community, the casino was a major source of income along with their Marquette location, but an ever-dwindling intake led the community to take a gamble themselves: they had recently invested nearly fifty million dollars into renovating the two Michigan establishments in hopes to stay competitive and attract more out-of-town money of a wealthier clientele. With the internet, those who just wanted to gamble—and didn't care about the ambiance or games played—didn't even have to leave their houses anymore.

While Marquette was getting the lion's share of the money for a complete overhaul in a brand new location, Baraga's interior and ventilation systems had been redone, including their forty hotel rooms and their full table service restaurant, for those that wanted something more than the bar and pub food available on the floor. The casino floor had been given a facelift, replacing the previously dim room—complete with smoke-stained walls and dingy carpet—with brand new flooring, features, and fixtures. The old slots were retired, and the rows of three hundred plus machines now featured the latest games. Even the pit was expanded—two-deck blackjack, roulette, craps, three, five, and seven-card poker, and Texas Hold 'em. In addition to the gaming, the casino had a bowling alley, an indoor pool with whirlpool and sauna, and banquet/conference space, and the entire facility was now 100% smoke-free. People could still pull up and park their RVs, but it was no longer a key selling point and now most called ahead for a reservation.

Martinez tidied the food wrappers and empty drink containers from the long trip before getting out and stretching her legs. She'd opted to drive from Detroit, which ended up being shorter than going to the airport, waiting for a short regional flight with a two-hour stopover in Chicago, renting a car, and driving to the casino. Logistics aside, the idea of having nine hours alone on the road was appealing, and the changing season was the perfect backdrop. She would have rather driven her Hellcat, but it was more sensible to rent something that could go off road—she didn't know where the investigation was going to take her and should anyone decide to run her plates, her cover would hold up.

She rolled her special issue luggage in through the casino entrance and was bombarded by the bright lights and wall of sound—bells, whistles, chimes, rings, and whirls coming from the slot machines. In one corner, they were calling live Bingo, and—from the buzzing excitement—someone was having a streak of luck at the craps table. Martinez stuck to the entry and looked around. While casino floors were designed to keep people in, there was usually some signage on the periphery to direct traffic. It wasn't long until a young woman dressed in black slacks and a red top approached her with a warm smile. Her Ojibwa Casino nametag identified her as Emma.

"Welcome to Ojibwa Casino Hotel Baraga," she said cheerfully. "You look a little lost. What can I help you find?"

Martinez politely returned the smile. "I have a reservation for a room, but I'm not sure where to check in."

"I'd be happy to help you with that," she replied and motioned for Martinez to follow. "Will you be staying with us long?"

"At least a few days, but my business may keep me longer," Martinez answered vaguely.

Emma's face lit up. "Oh, what do you do?"

"I'm a correspondent doing a piece about native traditions. The Upper Peninsula is blessed with a robust indigenous population," she added for credibility.

Emma stepped behind the long marble countertop that

doubled as customer service and hotel reception and logged into one of the empty stations. "What name is the reservation under?"

"Tracy Martin from the Institute of Tradition," Martinez replied.

Emma kept up her smile as her eyes darted to the screen, and she typed and scrolled with her mouse. "Ms. Martin, you are in one of our suites. Would you like to keep the charges on the Visa used during booking?"

"Sure," Martinez agreed.

Emma went on autopilot, going over the room number and handing the key card with the wifi password inside, all tucked into a cardboard folder advertising a complimentary twenty dollars of casino chips for hotel guests, redeemable at the window right next to customer service and hotel reception. "Enjoy your stay, and let us know if you need anything," she concluded.

Martinez followed Emma's directions and skirted the edge of the casino floor until she reached the other end and took a right. She tested her keycard on the pad and was granted access into the wing that held guest accommodations. After nine hours in the car, all she wanted was room service and a shower, but she still had some reading to do before her meeting with the Ojibwa liaison tomorrow afternoon.

Martinez did a quick sweep when she first entered her room and checked everything out. The bed was king-sized, the bathtub was a Jacuzzi, and there was an actual sitting room with a couch that could become a pullout bed. Last-minute travel did have its perks—she often stayed in the most expensive room at the hotel, even if she had to suffer the middle seat on plane rides more often than not. Much to her disappointment, they did not offer room service, but the booklet inside the room directed her to their restaurant, Lucky 7's, and the Press Box Bar & Grill, both conveniently located off the gaming floor.

Martinez put a simple ward on her luggage—the magical equivalent of a hair plastered across the door to see if anyone had entered the room while she was gone—and stowed her gear. Armed with her room key, ID, and gun, she went to rustle up some grub. She opted for the bar, figuring the service would be faster to get people back to their slots or the pit. Her instinct was proven correct, as the barman immediately took her to-go order and whisked it to the kitchen.

Casinos had always struck Martinez as strange—a twenty-four adult theme park where it was easy to lose track of time, appetite, and perspective. Her line of work had enough implicit danger that gambling as a pastime never really appealed to her, and the few times she had been to Vegas, she honestly went to see the shows and eat nice food—a side effect of the gentrification of gambling from its seedier days. She would only shift enough complimentary chips into real ones to get the perks and walk away.

Still, she admired the purity of purpose in the pit. People

at the tables were there to play games of chance, and it didn't matter that on the whole, the house always won. The belief that they could be the statistical anomaly that bucked the odds was beautiful in its own sad way, like a wilting cut flower that perked up when it got a little water…it was still dying, but not yet. She took the opportunity to redeem the voucher for her complimentary twenty dollars' worth of chips, and fifteen minutes later, she was heading back to her room, dinner in hand.

Martinez parked herself on the sofa with her food and reading—one downfall of driving was that she couldn't review case information during travel. She picked up where she'd left off: background information about the history and cultural legacy of the Ojibwa, also known as the Chippewa. Much to her surprise, many of the things she had assumed were racist stereotypes about Native Americans from the collective zeitgeist were legitimate practices of the Ojibwa.

The Ojibwa actually held pow-wows as communal ceremonies with drumming, dancing, and song. They really made dreamcatchers and intricate beadwork, and not just for sale to tourists. Their shamans sometimes used sweat lodges and shaking tents when acting as intermediaries between the people and the manitous, but there were many ways for helpers of the spirits to restore balance between the mind, body, spirit, and emotions. Each had their own way of accessing another realm through dreams, song, dance, and other rituals, just like practicing the esoteric arts was based on personal subconscious understanding.

The L'Anse Reservation was composed primarily of two non-contiguous sections on either side of the Keweenaw Bay in Baraga County. Even though there was a village called L'Anse, only part of it was on reservation land and many of the community events took place in the village of Baraga, which was entirely within the reservation's boundaries. Martinez logged onto the wifi and familiarized herself with some of the initiatives sponsored by the Keweenaw Bay Indian Community.

They held workshops on traditional foods and practices like drum circles, preparing tobacco, and plants found in indigenous gardens with recipes. In the summer, they held weekly farmers markets in both Baraga and L'Anse. There were clinics for traditional medicine, breastfeeding support, traditional pregnancy and childbirth practices, and cradleboard workshops. They also held informative meetings on topical interests that intersected their community like chronic wasting disease in the deer population and support for Native American veterans and youth. When Martinez saw the pasty sale fundraiser for veterans held earlier in the year, she cracked a smile. The Ojibwa may have been here first, but it seemed that they were just as much in love with the savory stuffed pasties as any other Yooper.

Martinez checked the time and was glad that she was still on target for an early night and a fresh start in the morning.

Figuring she had read enough not to put her foot in her mouth tomorrow, she put the files away and pulled up her map and the GPS coordinates. The first two attacks were within thirty minutes of the casino, but the most recent site was almost two hours away. She'd considered hitting it on her way in, but the sun had already set and she felt it unwise to wander the woods alone in the dark when something potentially supernatural was attacking hunters.

This time of year, daylight hours were on the decline, and she worked out the most efficient route to hit all three before returning to Baraga for her appointment with Eugene Stately, the Ojibwa contact for the Institute of Tradition. She laid out her clothes for tomorrow and hit the shower, letting the hot water wash over her.

Chapter Five

McMillian, Michigan, USA
20th of November, 10:15 a.m. (GMT-5)

Martinez parked on the shoulder of the country road and kept the heater running while she drank another cup of warm coffee from the thermos she'd filled at the casino bar before she left. The tables were closed for the morning but the casino was open twenty-four hours a day, and there was always alcohol and a fresh, hot pot of Joe to keep people at the slots, depending on their poison.

She'd already hit the first two locations and came up with the same magical signature at both sites. Unfortunately, it looked completely different from any of the manitou signatures Chloe and Dot had provided her, which only left the two-hour drive east to McMillian. Her plan was to approach the site where the two dead hunters were found from public land, and claim ignorance if she encountered the owner. It would attract less attention and questions than flashing her FBI badge.

She chewed a stick of jerky and washed it down with the last of the coffee in her cup. She systematically double-checked her gear before leaving the warmth of the Cherokee. Her saltcaster, disguised as a vape pen, was in one pocket and her phone with the GPS coordinates on silent in the other. Around her hips, she had her carbon fiber knife in its scabbard on her left and her Glock 43 was loaded with banishment bullets on her right. She'd double-socked for warmth, and damned if Weber wasn't right about the moccasins fitting her feet. She zipped up her hunter orange windbreaker, which just about concealed her hip holster when she stood.

Martinez cut off the engine and pulled her rifle from the backseat to complete the ruse. It was loaded, and she made sure the safety was on. She locked the vehicle and started hiking into the cool morning. She had inherited the rifle from her father, and even though it hadn't been used in over a decade, she kept it clean, oiled, and in good repair. She knew how to hunt deer, small game, and waterfowl, but it wasn't something she did for fun. It had been her father's thing, something he chose to do with her in their times together, much to her mother's consternation. Whenever her mother objected, he replied, "Pretty sure 'divorced' means you don't get to tell me how to spend time with my kid anymore, as long as I keep sending child support."

The truth was, he hadn't known what to do with a little girl, but Martinez didn't mind; she didn't always know how to be a little girl. So instead of buying her dolls and having tea parties, he brought her along on things he liked doing. The first summer after the divorce, they had gone fishing and he'd taught her what he knew—how to bait and cast a line, and to keep quiet in body and spirit so as to not spook the fish. When she got a nibble and pulled up a fry, he taught her to throw back the little ones so they had a chance to grow up and reproduce. When she'd finally caught something substantial—as long as her arm!—he showed her how to humanly stun a fish before bleeding it out. He'd expected her to cry, but she was more interested in asking questions and handling a knife, something her mother would have never let her do. She hadn't even complained when she had to gut and scale her own fish, and he'd considered it an unmitigated success.

Over the years, they'd developed a language of silence and intermittent instruction, and her time with her father became an outdoor adventure away from the vigilant eyes of her mother. When she'd turned ten, he bought her an airgun for Christmas—which her mother had refused to let her use until she was twelve. By the time she was thirteen, her father had showed her how to shoot a rifle. She remembered the bruise on her shoulder from the recoil, even though she stood and braced like he'd shown her. During her teen years, she started accompanying her father during hunting season into the mountainous woods of Colorado. While her classmates were figuring out how modify their uniforms to show more skin and sneak in makeup, she was learning how to field dress a deer and care for a rifle.

Technically, the jacket she was wearing was also her father's.

She'd gotten cold on the drive back and he'd given it to her to keep warm. She'd forgotten to give it back to him before she returned to her mother's, and he'd told her to keep it and bring it the next time she came out. Neither of them knew that would be their last hunting trip together. When they got the notification that he was killed in the line of duty, her mother took to her room for three days before making herself and Martinez presentable for the funeral.

The babble of a creek grew louder as Martinez followed her phone. She cautiously advanced—the moccasins might soften her step, but it wouldn't help much if she snapped a fallen branch. There were animal tracks leading to and away from the water, as well as footprints. Martinez visually swept the area, looking for signs of other hunters. There were no blinds or stands in place nor was there a hint of bright orange, camouflaged or otherwise. She cast out her will but found nothing supernaturally untoward. Only then did she step out from behind the trees into the clearing where the two hunters were attacked the previous week.

Martinez slung her rifle over her shoulder and retrieved her saltcaster, blowing a fine dust around her. She flipped the cartridge back to vape mode and waited for the salt to shake itself out. If anyone were to come upon her, she was just another hunter taking a smoke break. It took half a minute, but the white grains started to dance across the trampled leaf fall into two signatures—one was the same as the two previous sites and the other she recognized as manitou. Unfortunately, she couldn't recall if it was one of the good ones or one of the bad ones. She quick snapped pictures of both signatures and kicked the salt to disperse the magic.

She hustled back to the SUV before examining the pictures more closely. Without her laptop, she was left flipping back and forth between photos, unable to compare them side-by-side. Even in the best of circumstances, reading magical signatures could be tricky, like trying to find a match on fingerprints or facial recognition or actual handwritten signatures. There was a reason she generally sent signatures to the Mine for identification, although numerous agents had told her it got easier with practice.

To the best of her ability, she identified it as a female bear spirit, generally thought of as a protective manitou. Martinez sent off both signatures to the Salt Mine and started the two-hour drive back to Baraga. She ran the timeline in her head while she drove. The first attack was three weeks ago, and the second roughly ten days after that. She didn't understand the significance of a manitou only at the third scene, but she was about to meet with someone who might be able to shed some light on the situation.

Chapter Six

Baraga, Michigan, USA
20th of November, 1:00 p.m. (GMT-5)

Eugene Stately looked up from his desk when he heard the electronic chime of the front door opening. It took him a second to remember that the receptionist had called off sick this morning. He looked down at the time on his computer screen; somehow, the hour lunch break had zoomed past. Today, they were holding a traditional medicine clinic, and he had to get back to manning the reception desk and answering the phones. The Keweenaw Bay Indian Community Health System had limited office staff, which meant everyone had to be capable of wearing many hats, however ill fitting.

"*Boozhoo!*" he called out. "I'll be with you in just a minute." He scanned the screen and rechecked the cells before clicking submit on his request for supplies. When he rounded the corner, he caught sight of a pretty young woman sitting patiently in one of the chairs. He didn't recognize her as one of the clinic's regular visitors and approached gently. At six-foot-two, he was a big man and didn't want to scare her off. "Can I help you?"

Martinez rose and addressed him, "I'm Tracy Martin. I have

an appointment with Eugene Stately."

He suddenly remembered the appointment with the Institute of Tradition that he'd made just yesterday morning. After the morning he'd had, it completely slipped his mind. "That would be me," he replied and extended his hand.

She firmly shook it and quickly sized him up as a gentle giant that lived up to his surname—a tall, broad-shouldered, barrel-chested marine turned community organizer in his late fifties. He was dressed in jeans and a buttoned-down shirt with no tie, and the vexed expression on his face told her that all was not well. She smiled and threaded out her will as she started the typical pleasantries, "I really appreciate you agreeing to meet with me on such short notice. I'm really excited to cover how Ojibwa celebrate autumn and how the community handles the Thanksgiving celebration."

His face softened. "No problem at all," he said gregariously, "but I'm afraid things are a little chaotic today. We're short one very capable woman, and I'm afraid I'm a poor substitute. Would it be possible for us to meet later today?"

"Certainly. I'm staying at the casino. We can talk after work, if that would be better," she graciously offered.

"That would be fine," he replied with relief. He didn't want to disappoint her—she had come all this way to speak with him.

Martinez spun out a little more of her will. "Is there someone else you would recommend that I talk to this afternoon—

perhaps someone with intimate knowledge of traditional stories and ceremonies? I would really like to capture how the Ojibwa use rituals to connect the people to the sources of life in this time of bounty."

Stately wracked his brain on who would be available and willing to speak to Ms. Martin on such short notice that would also be a good ambassador of the community. "There may be someone. Let me make a phone call." Martinez nodded and took a seat, reeling out her will as he went back to his office, just like her father had taught her how to keep a fish on the line.

*****

Martinez parked her SUV opposite the double-wide sitting on its concrete piling. Its blue siding was worn but clean, and the wind chimes hanging on the front tinkled in the breeze. The table and stack of plastic chairs on the porch were covered, and the small garden was turned over for the winter. She climbed out of the driver's seat and felt the whole neighborhood's eyes on her from behind their curtains as she climbed up the three steps to the porch. She wasn't sure if was because she was a stranger, or because this house rarely got visitors.

Martinez heard a dog barking from within before she even rang the doorbell, but she followed custom and pressed the button. She heard a stern voice command the dog to sit before Rosaline Stillwater opened the door. She was a doughy elderly woman with a round face, but her demeanor was stark and lean, like the form of a racing greyhound. Martinez put on her best smile and introduced herself. "Hello, I'm Tracy Martin, a correspondent for the Institute of Tradition. Eugene Stately said you might be willing to talk to me about some of the tribal customs and ceremonies."

Stillwater nodded tersely and turned around, leaving the door open for Martinez. She cast out her will, checking for wards, and found something present on the wreath hanging on the door—either her host was a magician or she knew one. Martinez stepped over the threshold and closed the door behind her to keep the heat and the dog from getting out. She followed Stillwater around a corner, and found a very excited Yorkshire Terrier whose tail wagged furiously despite the fact that it was obediently sitting on his haunches. "Hello, sweetie," Martinez's voice went up an octave and put her hand out for the dog to smell. "Are you a good dog?"

"That's Pickles," Stillwater answered curtly. "Because that's his favorite food." The woman watched to see what her dog made of the visitor—he had a good nose for sniffing out bad apples. Even though Martinez had washed her hands since, Pickles picked up the beef jerky she had eaten earlier. He cautiously smelled past it to see if it was safe before licking her hand and pressing his cold wet nose against her. Stillwater marginally relaxed—she'd passed the door *and* the Pickles test.

"I don't suppose I could use your bathroom before we get

started," Martinez asked apologetically. "I've had a bit more coffee than I should have this morning."

"Down the hall, second door to your left," Stillwater informed her. Martinez nodded, and wondered who would win in a staring contest: Leader or Stillwater. Martinez really did have to use the bathroom, but it also provided her an opportunity to salt and confirm that Stillwater was a practitioner. According to Stately, she lived alone in the house after her kids moved away and her husband died.

Martinez sat on the toilet, waiting for the blown salt to form a pattern, and snapped a picture once one emerged. It had to be one of the more awkward bathroom experiences she'd had in a while. She turned on the faucet and wiped the floor with a damp section of clean toilet paper, picking up as much of the fine salt as she could. Stillwater struck her as the kind of person who would notice a little salt on the floor—what Martinez had seen of her house so far was immaculate.

She flushed the evidence down the commode and washed her hands. When she returned, Stillwater had tea set up in the sitting room with cookies set out. Pickles was contently chewing on a milk-bone by her feet. She silently motioned for Martinez to take a seat on the couch wrapped in plastic. It had been a nice sofa when it was purchased forty years ago, and the plastic was slightly discolored from all the smoke that had accumulated over years of smoking and smudging.

Martinez took a seat and the plastic squeaked as the cushion below depressed. "Is this tea for me?" she asked before taking a cup. Stillwater nodded in the affirmative. Martinez politely took a sip and was pleasantly surprised at how nice it was—strong and sweet, but not cloyingly so. "Thank you. It's nice to have something warm on such a cold day."

"You say your name is Tracy Martin, but you are no marten," Stillwater spoke bluntly.

Martinez swallowed another sip as she tried to parse her host's meaning. Was she flat-out questioning Martinez's alias and pretense? Unlikely, as she had deliberately not used her will to curry favor with Stillwater. She pulled up what she had read last night—there was a marten clan among the Ojibwa. Was Stillwater trying to say that she wasn't one of them? Martinez set down her cup in the saucer and chose her phrasing deliberately, showing that she understood some of the Ojibwa's ways. "That is the name I was given, but is not my true name," she answered honestly without giving anything away.

This answer pleased Stillwater, who took up her teacup and nudged the plate of cookies toward Martinez. "And what does this Tracy not-marten want with me?"

Who would Stately have sent me to if I hadn't charmed him? Martinez marveled as she took a cookie and dipped it into her tea, which was the wrong move according to her host's face. *Stillwater is not a dunker*, she noted as she bit the offending wet portion off and placed the rest of the cookie on the side of her saucer. Chloe and Dot's primer said to be truthful if she was going to approach a traditional practitioner, and the woman sitting opposite her was the sort to smell bullshit a mile away. "I need to contact a manitou and ask her some questions, and I believe you are capable of such a feat."

Stillwater sat back in her seat; she was not expecting honesty up front. "What manidoo do you wish to speak to?" she asked curiously, using the Ojibwe pronunciation.

"A noozhe-makwa manidoo," Martinez replied, repeating the Ojibwa name associated with the signature that Chloe and Dot had confirmed less than an hour ago. Stillwater almost smiled at hearing her guest speak in her native language, and Martinez was glad she had taken the time to learn the phonetic alphabet. Unfortunately, the twins were still working on the other signature, which made the momma bear of the woods her best bet at getting answers. "I believe she has encountered something dangerous in the woods, and it is my duty to restore balance by removing it."

Martinez placed a baggie of the asema on the table. It was roughly half of what Weber had given her, just in case she had to make another request at a later time. She knew it was important to tell Stillwater exactly what was required before offering her the sacred tobacco, essentially giving her the option of refusing. If the woman accepted the offering, it was a done deal. Martinez felt Stillwater poke and prod her with her will, looking for an in, so she summoned her will and parried her probe. Wordlessly, they magically sized each other up, like fencers tapping tips.

Pickles raised his head from his bone and looked around, ears perked.

"Are you on your moontime?" Stillwater inquired.

"No," Martinez replied simply. "How about you?" she joked nonchalantly.

The numerous lines on her tanned face gained dimension as a broad smile came across the older woman's face and her cheeks blossomed as a full-bodied laugh left her lips. Her posture relaxed, and Pickles resumed his assault on the milk-bone. Stillwater picked up the bag and examined the contents. She rubbing the mix in her wrinkled hands, smelling the blend. "Did you prepare this?" she asked with equal parts respect and suspicion.

"No, but the Institute of Tradition respects the old ways. *All* old ways," Martinez emphasized.

Stillwater put the offering back in its bag and sealed it shut. She didn't need much time to deliberate; she was a woman who knew her mind. "Come tonight at nine, and we will try to communicate with the spirit world. Come with an open heart. No drugs or alcohol until then," she instructed. She pocketed the asema and finished her tea with Martinez in amicable silence.

Chapter Seven

Baraga, Michigan, USA
20th of November, 6:07 p.m. (GMT-5)

Eugene Stately entered Lucky 7's through the casino and spotted Tracy Martin sitting at one of the booths against the wall of windows. He strode over and made his apologies, "I'm sorry I'm late. It took a while to shut everything down at the end of the day." He took off his jacket and hat before sliding onto the cobalt blue vinyl seat opposite her.

"Not a problem," Martinez reassured him as she locked her phone's screen and put it away. "I was just going over some notes."

There was a menu waiting for him on the table, but he didn't need it—he'd eaten here enough times to know what he was getting. Lucky 7's served standard American cuisine with weekend dinner specials: Friday fish fry, Saturday BBQ ribs, and Sunday roast beef. Because the casino never closed, neither did the restaurant, and on any given holiday, they featured courses and desserts not typically found on the menu. It was solidly good food at a good price, although they'd jazzed up the menu—and the prices—when the interior was updated.

Stately placed his menu at the edge of the table on top of Martinez's, the universal sign to waitstaff that the table is ready to order. "How was your visit with Ms. Stillwater?" he asked curiously.

Martinez made a dubious face. "I think I passed, but I can't be sure."

He chuckled at her response. She could see why he was the liaison to the Institute of Tradition. He was very open and expressive in comparison to most of the people she had interacted with in town, barring casino staff that were paid to be gregarious. The actual residents of Baraga were terse by nature and didn't dole out excessive praise. They reminded her more of a Minnesotan than the standard Yooper. Things were either fine or not, and you wouldn't catch them waxing poetic on the *amazing* sandwich they'd had at lunch. Contrary to the popular and persistent myth of the stoic Indian, it wasn't hard to make an Ojibwa smile; there just had to be something to smile about.

"That's my fault. I don't like not keeping my promises, but hopefully she wasn't too hard on you. Let me buy you a drink to make up for it," he offered, noting her empty glass.

"Sadly, a Shirley Temple for me," Martinez lamented. "I'm seeing Ms. Stillwater after dinner, and she was very firm about no alcohol in the meantime."

"She invited you back?" he said with genuine surprise and a hint of admiration. "Well then, I would say you definitely passed." He flagged down a waitress and she took their order: a beer and burger for the gentleman and another Shirley Temple and steak with a salad for the lady. After their drinks arrived, he settled in with his beer. "So, you're a reporter with the Institute of Tradition," he opened.

"They call them correspondents, but yes," Martinez replied.

"And you want to write an article about the Ojibwa in Michigan," he confirmed the facts as he knew them.

"That's right. I was hoping to learn more about the rituals and ceremonies performed in autumn. There is growing interest in understanding the Native American perspective this time of year," Martinez answered, alluding to growing awareness of the legacy of colonization in light of how Native Americans are portrayed at Thanksgiving, and the fact that the US is still celebrating Columbus Day in a time when parts of the south were taking down their Confederate statues.

He wrinkled his brow at her turn of phrase. "The Keweenaw Bay Indian Community has no problem with you documenting and reporting our customs for a larger audience, but I am concerned at how that information will be conveyed," he spoke seriously. "This is very much how *we* do things, and that may not be true of other tribes. Heck, it may not even be the way Ojibwa in Minnesota do it. It would be a disservice to everyone to present our ceremonies and rituals in a monolithic way."

Martinez was taken aback at his earnest commitment that

she get it right, and found it endearing that he used a minced oath instead of cursing. "I think I understand. There is more than one way to be Native American, and sloppy presentation, no matter how well intentioned, can cause more damage than good."

His brow unfurled as his face relaxed. "We're not here to shame anyone with 1/16 indigenous blood into living a traditional life or to move back to the reservation, but we also can't ignore the comprehensive and deliberate effort to erase our culture. We have generational gaps where our language, crafts, ceremonies, songs, dances, and history have been wiped out. We just want to make traditional ways an option again, and that's why our focus is on intergenerational interaction."

"And that's why people like Ms. Stillwater are so important to the community," she concluded.

"Exactly," he said, and tipped his beer toward her. "She can be surly, but she is generous with her knowledge, which is why I sent you to her. Knowing where we come from culturally is the foundation of decolonization."

It was the same story throughout history, all over the globe: the colonizer's blueprint. If one wanted to take over a place that was already populated, one had to either eradicate the local culture or integrate them into the colonial one. Integration was the harder task, because the colonizer had to win over the local populace to have them embrace the new ways. Eradication was brutal on the indigenous populace but easier on the colonizer;

it meant separating the local people from their roots and demonizing native customs.

The actual methods that took place were variations on a theme. Making it illegal or punishable to speak one's native language or practice one's religion was a common play, even in the modern day. The economics of colonization disrupted the stability of their livelihood and community structure while simultaneously creating a social and fiscal bias against natives and, de facto, their traditions. If it got to the point where members of the native community rejected their traditional ways in hopes of an easier road, the colonizers simply had to wait out the clock. How many generations did it take to lose a language? How long before their history was forgotten?

"And the fact that it makes white people nervous when you use terms like 'decolonization' is just a bonus?" she needled him with a sly, subtle smile.

"Recognizing and reversing colonization is painful for everyone," he replied diplomatically. "But serendipity comes in many forms."

Martinez sipped her sweetened pink ginger ale and murmured conspiratorially, "So, can I ask you a personal question, off the record?" He nodded his consent. "What's *your* take on Thanksgiving?"

His gave a grin, aware that he was on tricky ground. "I think it is very telling that Americans need a holiday to remind themselves to be thankful. For an Ojibwa who follows the teachings of the seven grandfathers, it is integral to living—like breathing or eating. We give thanks to Mother Earth for all things that sustain us. We recognize and honor the sacrifice that another living thing has made to sustain us, be that fish, deer, gathered plants, or harvested crops. In that respect, Thanksgiving is just another day to me. But if it's a paid holiday that gives me more time to spend with my family and community, I'm okay with that."

Martinez nodded with a new appreciation for her eloquently spoken dinner companion. "Speaking of being thankful—food incoming," she gave him a head's up as the laden tray came their way. "Something tells me I'm going to need all the energy I can get, because Ms. Stillwater isn't the sort to pull punches."

"Are you sure you aren't Ojibwa?" he teased her.

"I'm Latina—there's a Ms. Stillwater on every block."

Chapter Eight

Martinez returned to Stillwater's home with five minutes to spare, and this pleased the medicine woman. She appreciated someone who was punctual; not only did it show consideration and thoughtfulness, it was evidence of a mind that could effectively execute a plan. She called her petitioner to the backyard, where she had been busy since their visit earlier that afternoon.

The shaking tent had a storied reputation and was used for a variety of rituals, but for Stillwater, it was the best way to contact the spirit world. The not-marten wasn't looking for healing, a blessing, or divination; she was looking for an audience with a powerful manidoo. She'd unearthed the frame of her jiisakaan and covered it in its cured hide. Custom dictated that the structure must be entered in the dark, but she'd readied the inside to receive the fire. She'd ritually cleansed herself and donned her sacred clothing from the cedar chest in the guest bedroom. Then, she'd applied her colors on her face and body and packed up the ritual components—including Martinez's asema—in a sacred bundle.

Martinez sized up the tent, which was domed at the top instead of the iconic teepee shape. It was six feet tall and three feet in diameter—big enough for the two of them, but only just. In the backyard, a fire glowed in the sunken pit, although no smoke came out of the narrow circular opening at the top of the tent.

Martinez approached the medicine woman and presented her with a token of her thanks selected with Stately's help: a lined beaver-print Slanket, a package of maple creams that happened to be Stillwater's favorite brand, and a smoked pig ear for Pickles, who was visiting one of the neighbors for the evening. She accepted the gifts and sat Martinez down by the fire.

The gleam in Stillwater's eyes belied her excitement despite her impassive mien. It had been a long time since someone called upon her practice, as if somehow age and widowhood could rob her of her skills. None of her children followed her in the arts, content to leave their ancestral homeland and regard their heritage as a colorful background for their otherwise modern, American lives.

The medicine woman picked up a bowl of paint, and Martinez stilled while Stillwater applied streaks of white to her face—the color of peace. The slight tremor in her hand disappeared as she focused on the strokes, and she prepared Martinez on what was to come. "The ritual will start when we enter the tent with the fire. We will circle the tent four times before lighting the fire within. Then, I will burn your offering and begin my song to call the spirit helpers to aid us in finding your noozhe-makwa. Your job will be to concentrate your spirit and keep the beat with the rattle drum. You just roll it back and forth between your hands. If we make contact, I will tell you when you may speak. Once it starts, we don't leave the tent until the passage between worlds has been closed and the ritual is over. Do you understand?"

"Yes," Martinez verbally confirmed. She'd sent a message to the Salt Mine beforehand just in case things went terribly wrong, but she had some protective measures in place. No one had said anything against her wearing the amber amulet that protected her from being targeted by magic. Additionally, she had her Glock loaded with banishment bullets discreetly concealed on her person. Having an open heart didn't mean walking in unarmed.

Stillwater carried her sacred bundle in her left hand so that it would be closer to her heart, and picked up a fire starter from the pit. Martinez held the flap open, and they entered into the dark tent. Stillwater began singing, and Martinez followed her as she perambulated four times. Then, the older woman ignited the dried wood within the circle of stones at the tent's center. Once the flames took hold, they sat on the ground beside each other, making space for the manidoo to join them.

The medicine woman opened her sacred bundle and rolled

everything out just so. She handed Martinez the rattle drum, and Martinez started to roll the well-worn handle between her hands in time with Stillwater's song. The fragrant cedar wood crackled as Stillwater added the tobacco to the fire, and she pulled out a smudge of sage. *Hail Mary, full of grace...* Martinez summoned her will and faithfully kept the beat.

In Ojibwe, Stillwater called to the earth that held them, to the moon that gave women their power to create life, to the eagle spirit who saw all with its keen eyes from soaring heights. She petitioned them in the name of peace, enticing them with the sweet fragrance of the smoke and her lyrical song. It was a small petition: help in locating the female bear spirit who protects the woods. Martinez didn't need to understand the words to get the gist of the request.

Martinez lost track of time in the repetition, but she focused her will on Stillwater's voice, the smoke, and the drone of the rattle. Then, she felt a tug on the web of will she had woven inside the tent. Something was there with them, and Stillwater perceived it as well. The hide and frame of the dome started to shake and rattle, and the medicine woman changed her litany. She addressed the spirits, asking on behalf of Martinez to speak with noozhe-makwa, imparting her desire to help restore balance in the woods.

As the tent calmed, Martinez felt something touch her hand and still her rattle, but it wasn't Stillwater. The drumming stopped, as did the song, and a voice spoke through the smoky tent. "Why have you called the mother bear from her patrol?" Stillwater nodded her head for Martinez to speak.

"Great noozhe-makwa, I seek information about the creature that hunts man in the forest," Martinez stated plainly.

The haze considered her statement. "The forest is full of predators. Why do you take note of this hunter?"

The photos of the mutilated bodies crossed her mind's eye, and she remembered Stately's words at dinner. "Because it takes life without honoring the sacrifice." Martinez's answer resonated with the medicine woman and the manidoo.

"It is true that creatures of insatiable hunger have recently entered the wood," the manidoo admitted.

Martinez picked up on the plural, but proceeded with her preplanned questions. "Are they wendigoes?" she wagered a guess after mentally scrolling through the usual suspects in this area.

The smoke scoffed at her suggestion. "I am familiar with them and they with me," the bear modestly boasted. "No, this is something unknown to me. An interloper from afar. They hunt like coyotes but look like cougars, only larger. Their razor claws tear through flesh effortlessly, their fangs are sharp and vicious, and they stalk their prey for the sport of it."

"Do you know when they arrived?" Martinez inquired.

"Kitchi-Sabe saw them crossing through the middle lands before entering the forest on the night the Hunter's Moon hid half its light," the gauzy bear answered. The thought of sasquatch roaming the Magh Meall of the Upper Peninsula in the moonlight would have otherwise delighted Martinez, but her focus was on the case. *The Hunter's Moon—aka the Blood Moon—is in October, and November's full moon was last week...* Martinez reasoned. Which meant they had been here about a month, and there had already been four confirmed dead.

"How many hunt in the pack?" she queried.

"There are as many as there are moons in a solar circuit," the noozhe-makwa answered.

There are twelve of them?! Martinez processed her answer. "Did they all come at once, or are more coming as time passes?"

"The eagle has not seen more," the ursine-shaped haze rippled as it spoke.

Martinez searched for the right phrasing and settled with, "I caught your scent at their most recent feeding, where two men were killed, but not at the two previous sites closer to here."

The manidoo was nothing more than vapor and mist, but it felt like she stood on her hind legs and postured wide. "I protect my domain, but I am one in a vast forest. The eagle may see all, but it can only land one perch at a time."

"I meant no offense, great noozhe-makwa," Martinez quickly humbled herself. "Forgive my imprecise language. I ask because if you have obtained a piece of them, I may be able to track them and send them to their true home."

The bear addressed Stillwater in Ojibwe, "Are you sure she

is not a marten?"

"She had not been named. Nothing is certain," the medicine woman answered honestly.

The noozhe-makwa gathered smoke between her ethereal paws and compressed it until it took solid form. A long, sharp incisor fell to the ground from thin air. "There *were* thirteen," the spirit explained. Her giant paw rested on Martinez's head; it was both heavy and weightless. "You have my blessing, maybe-marten. The spirit of the forest is with you. Finish this quickly and return the balance to the woods." Martinez felt a surge through the baseline will she had exerted for the ritual.

"Thank you for your boon, great noozhe-makwa," Martinez responded in gratitude.

Stillwater touched Martinez's arm, and she resumed spinning the rattle drum once more. The medicine woman started a new song, one extolling the might, wisdom, and honor of the manidoo. She gave thanks to Mother Earth and the moon, and reiterated the commitment of those within the tent to heal the wounds inflicted upon the forest. The tent quivered again, this time a mere tremor, and the two women were alone again.

Stillwater put out the fire and meticulously repacked her sacred bundle. Martinez took out a clean bag and scooped up the tooth from the ground. The warmth and smoke within the tent rapidly escaped as soon as Stillwater opened the flap to the outside. Martinez took a seat by the fire pit, processing what she had just seen. It was unlike anything she had experienced so far in her magical education. There was no hollow summoning circle, no elaborate ruins, no trapping or binding of the spirit. It was like riding a wild stallion—untamed and free, but also precarious.

Stillwater took a seat next to Martinez, opened the package of maple creams, and offered her one. Her body's response to the rush of sugar told her they had been in there a while. "You've got a dangerous journey ahead of you," she remarked as she produced a flask and held it out toward Martinez.

"I thought I wasn't supposed to drink alcohol," she objected.

"The ritual's over," Stillwater declared and took a swig. When she offered it to Martinez one more time, she didn't say no.

Martinez washed off her face in the bathroom and stayed long enough to help Stillwater disassemble the tent and fold the hide. She thanked the medicine woman for her help and left her a stack of bills, courtesy of the Institute of Tradition. Stillwater accepted the payment and wished the maybe-marten luck in her hunt.

It was late by the time Martinez returned to her suite at the casino. She checked her messages, but there was still no word from Chloe and Dot on the signature. She kept the tooth in a box packed with salt for safekeeping and put in a request for the compass, a useful piece of kit Weber had improved since Wilson tested the prototype in the field. It was essentially a homing device for the supernatural—if you put a piece of magic in the back, the needle would point you in the direction of the source of that magic.

Being able to track these creatures was a start, but their location wasn't her biggest dilemma—there were a lot of them and one of her. By her reckoning, they were steadily moving east across the Upper Peninsula and killed roughly every ten days, which means they were due to feed any day now. The first two attacks were within thirty minutes of L'Anse Bay, and if her hypothesis was right, their next kill would be near McMillan by water.

To add to her list of concerns, she had her doubts on whether the banishment bullets she had would even work on them. She'd packed standard North American bullets as well as the ones Weber had given her for Native American coverage. The four sigils etched in gold were culturally significant symbols from the largest discrete indigenous groups, since many tribes north of Mesoamerica didn't have a codified written script until the last couple of hundred years,

However, the fact that the noozhe-makwa manidoo didn't recognize them was less than reassuring—if the creatures didn't subtextually understand the notion of banishment inscribed on the bullets, the missile wouldn't exile them out of the mortal realm and back to their native home. It would be like someone telling Martinez to "go home" in Finnish—it wouldn't mean anything to her, because she didn't speak the language.

And then there was the implication that they must have traveled from their middle lands into the Upper Peninsula's middle lands, which—according to her understanding—was impossible. Every place had an in between zone, created by the fae, a realm with points loosely tethered to the mortal realm, what the Salt Mine generically called the Magh Meall. Except there wasn't just one Magh Meall; there were many that existed simultaneously in a non-Euclidean geography that defied mapping. That's why Martinez had to go to Greece to enter the Greek Magh Meall to retrieve the waters of Narcissus in August—Magh Mealls don't connect.

Martinez reported her findings to the Salt Mine in hopes that they would come up with something by the morning. *Maybe Hobgoblin could come and blow them up if I could find their lair?* She grasped at straws in a fit of tired desperation.

Martinez peeled off her clothes and crashed into bed, too exhausted for a shower. Her hair was infused with the smell of tobacco, cedar, sage, and sweet grass, and she dreamt of a great bear spirit, patrolling the forest while she slept.

Chapter Nine

Newberry, Michigan, USA
20th of November, 11:40 p.m. (GMT-4)

Jacob Reeves adjusted the vents as he waited for the traffic light to change; it was a cold night and the layers of clothing he wore were strategically chosen for disrobing, not for warmth. He followed his phone's prompts to the address of his gig—a bachelorette party.

He hadn't done one in a while, but once upon a time, bachelorette parties were his bread and butter. When he couldn't get booked for stage time at the club, there was always someone getting married that wanted some personal attention before they tied the knot. In his experience, the rowdiness of the roaming bachelorette party that stumbled into the club was blessedly absent at private parties—clients engaging him were paying a premium to keep the riff raff out of their event, and they were generally tamer than what the movies would suggest.

After he had figured out how to work exotic dancing into a profession instead of a side gig that got him a lot of tail, he found himself mostly performing for men—not because he was bisexual or gay, but because they paid better, say nothing of bachelor parties for gay men. When he was initially contacted for a bachelorette party, he was reluctant to drive this far into the boonies until he saw the number of zeros in the offer— cash, half at booking, half upon completion, plus whatever got stuffed in his thong by the end of the night. He got the impression that this was being sold to everyone else as a bucolic midweek getaway with the girls, instead of one last hurrah happening off the books. The pay was high enough that he'd felt the need to clarify that he didn't have sex with his clients, and he'd been assured that wouldn't be a problem.

He'd asked if they had a preference on his persona. He had accumulated a vast array of costumes over the years; thanks to his excellent tailor—any pair of pants could be turned into rip-aways if they were bought two sizes too big and cut along the seam with Velcro sewn in. Most were physical jobs or men in uniforms, like a sexy cop, firefighter, sailor, soldier, cowboy, or construction worker, but he'd also been asked to assume more cranial roles, like a sexy scientist, doctor, academic, or librarian. Sometimes people just wanted him to look like the average guy off the street, and there were a surprising number of requests for him to knock on the door as a repairman or a pizza delivery guy. It always struck him as a little sad that when given the chance to have their ultimate fantasy come to life, so many women just wanted someone who could fix things or bring them food.

This party had asked for clean cut with no body hair, which

Jacob interpreted as businessman. He'd opted for a pinstriped suit with wool overcoat and fedora hat, because it had plenty of parts and pieces to remove as his dance progressed—the jacket, the tie, the buttoned-down shirt, and of course, the tear-away pants. He went with Armani boxer briefs with a thong underneath, just to put in another reveal when they wanted a little more skin. The hat either came of first or last, depending on the routine.

Truth be known, his clients—male or female—didn't really pay too much attention to the clothes, but what was underneath them. He'd been blessed with a large cock, but he'd worked hard for the rest and being a gymhead wasn't enough. Being hot and wiggling only got a stripper so far, and in order to quit his day job, he'd had to step up his game.

On top of his normal workout, he did isolation exercises and worked on his flexibility so he could do the show-stopping acrobatics that really worked up the crowd, like dolphin dives, monkey jumps, and handstands. He learned to not take himself so seriously and how to read the room. He watched other dancers and dissected their routines: how to be dynamic, hold interest, pick the right music, and excite the crowd with a well-placed hip thrust or body roll timed to the beat. There was a lot more to it than taking your clothes off.

The stakes were even higher at private engagements. In the clubs, performers rotated through the night, and his segment was fifteen minutes, tops. He would work the room, do lap or floor dances once he found the right volunteers, and get off the stage to give the next guy a chance to make his money. It was completely different for private parties. Oftentimes, he was the only stripper, and they weren't going to have a variety of men like they would in a club. He earned his pay by performing for thirty to sixty minutes, and giving plenty of personal attention to the guests, especially the bride.

Jacob pulled into a gravel lot next to the powered-down party bus. The outside was decorated with strings of lights, signs, and balloons, and the theme was decidedly phallic. *Well, I've definitely got the right place*, he wryly thought before psyching himself up for whatever waited for him on the other side of the door. It could be anything from silly and playful to raunchy and handsy, and the presence of the bride's mother, aunties, and grandmother didn't always correlate with the former.

From the backseat, Jacob pulled out his briefcase, which held his mobile sound system, and lined up the app on his phone that would start the music. Then he unbuttoned his overcoat, donned his fedora, and flashed himself a smile in his rearview mirror. "Show time," he said aloud before exiting his vehicle.

*****

"I love you guys!" Lin slurred her words and haphazardly

cast out her arms to grab her companions in a hug.

"Maybe we overdid it on the drinks…" Mei whispered to Faye as she caught Lin mid-embrace. Faye giggled as she took another sip from her cocktail.

"Can I be honest with you guys?" Lin whisper-shouted. "I don't know if I can go through with this. What if I'm not ready?"

"Don't be silly," Faye chided her. "You're just nervous. And drunk."

Popo traded Lin's drink for water and rubbed her back, like she'd done when she was upset as a child. "Everyone has cold feet at the last minute. It's totally normal," she said soothingly.

Lin started to blubber. "What if I get up there and make a fool of myself in front of everybody?" She threw her hands up in the air, and they indelicately dropped like lead weights onto her lap. Popo gave Mei and Faye sharp looks for boozing up Lin on an empty stomach—of course it went right to her head!

Faye feigned an innocent look while Mei tried her hand at talking sense into their inebriated friend. "Lin, you're not thinking straight. The stripper will be here any minute, and then you can have something to eat. Things will look better once you have a little fun and get a little food in you."

"You don't want to disappoint everyone," Popo threw in some guilt for good measure. "Everyone has worked so hard to make this perfect for you."

Lin processed their words, albeit at a slower pace than

normal due to the alcohol. "Well, I am hungry."

"That's the spirit!" Faye applauded her. "Now get out there and enjoy your party. Don't let those other bitches get first hands on *your* stripper."

Lin gave a goofy grin but allowed herself to be led out to the center of the room to the cheers of all the females in her life. Tonight was her night.

A hush fell over the crowd as the door opened, and Jacob strode into the room—chest out, shoulders back. The inside was more intimate and charming than its rustic exterior suggested, and the dim lighting with a red tint gave it a slightly seedy feel. There would be no naughty "pin the tail on the donkey" at this gathering.

He tested the floor with his black, hard-soled Bruno Maglis—plenty of slide for him to dance and make full use of the knee pads under his trousers. His steps echoed amid the quiet murmuring; they were sizing him up, and based on their hungry eyes and enigmatic smiles, he passed muster. Jacob took off his overcoat and gave them a good look at the cut of his body under the fine threads—wide at the shoulders, slim through the waist, full through the buttocks, with strong, powerful thighs. "I'm looking for Ms. Lin Kwan," he enunciated each syllable with precision—everyone hated hearing their name butchered.

Lin felt a cluster of hands propel her forward. "I'm her," she answered in a higher register than normal. "What can I do for you?" she asked coquettishly.

He put his briefcase down on the table, speaker pointing out, and pulled out a chair for her. "If you'd take a seat, I believe I have something I can do for you."

She accepted his invitation and sat with her hands folded on her lap and ankles crossed and tucked to one side. She stared up at him with expectant eyes and he cued the music. He glided across the floor, sizing up the crowd—a dozen women in total. When he passed by the bride, he dramatically took off his hat and placed it lightly on her head. It canted to one side, but he could still see her eyes watching him from under the brim.

Jacob shrugged his suit jacket off his sculpted arms, punctuating its removal with a rapid triple hip thrust and roll of the chest to the beat. The early cheers let him know which among them were the rowdy ones, and where the bride fell on the spectrum. Lin wasn't hooting and hollering, but she didn't turn away from his gyrating body. Demure but curious...*I can work with that*, Jacob thought as he flung his tie away.

Were the bride a little more adventuresome, he would have used it as a binding or a blindfold, but he was going to have to coax this one out of her shell. He danced and rubbed himself up against a few guests while he unbuttoned his shirt, giving Lin a little more time to get comfortable but staying in her line of sight. Once his shirt was off, he popped his chest three times before doing a full body roll. He ran his hands down his torso as it undulated, ending with a crotch grab and simultaneous hip thrust. That elicited more of a response from everyone in the room, bride included.

Then he leapt into the air and twisted his body, using the momentum to dive to the ground and roll the front side of his body in an arch. Successfully transitioned to the floor, Jacob posed on all fours, butt out. The heady roar was deafening, and even Lin joined in. She gave him a mischievous grin that invited him to get closer. His biceps throbbed as he grinded the floor, his hips moving up and down, knees flowing in and out. Each thrush pushed him closer toward his target, and he stalked her like prey.

Then, in one fluid motion, he put down one hand and propelled himself into a back flip, landing on his feet. Everyone was surprised with his agility, but they clapped and yelled once they recovered. He straddled Lin, rolling his entire body in front of her and grinding his hips against her. He took her hands in his and guiding them to his naked chest. Her pulse quickened as he ran her hands up and down his washboard abs. She started laughing and screaming with the rest of group.

Jacob gave her a breather as he danced on a few other laps, including an older woman who slyly slapped him on the butt like he was a naughty schoolboy for shoving his groin against her. He spun around and took a few steps forward to make sure they could all have a good look before he bent down and ripped off his pants. Even the conservative ones in the back stood up and shouted once he was strutting around in just his underwear. He shimmied, tugging on the edge his boxer briefs, and teasing them with the top of the thong that was underneath. He stopped in front of Lin with his back to her and slid his Armanis down, giving her first view of his bare buttocks.

While he was crouched with his hands on the ground, he picked up his legs and wrapped them around the back of the chair. He writhed and shook his bare ass on her lap, and Lin gave it a few good whacks at the crowd's encouragement. He came out of the pose and knelt before Lin, who looked like she weighed one hundred and twenty pounds at most, and lifted the entire chair up.

She instinctively wrapped her arms around his neck and her legs around his torso, and Jacob let the chair fall back once he had a good grip on her. He pressed her again the wall, popping her hips up with his hands and thrusting against her to the rhythm of the music. His breathing was heavy from the exertion, and she could smell his natural scent cutting through his cologne. Her eyes widened, and her body arched in anticipation.

The women started whistling and cheering her name in the simulated act of sex, and she heard Faye's voice cut through the din. "Lin, stop playing with your food!" The other women laughed, although Jacob wasn't sure why. He was too busy concentrating on not dropping the bride when he saw her brown almond eyes enlarge. Her perfectly round pupils turn into vertical slits, and the whites of her eyes changed to a sallow green. Before he could react, Lin sank her teeth into his neck and tore off a chunk of flesh, severing his jugular vein in the process.

Jacob fell to the floor, and Lin landed on top of him, lapping up the warm sanguine fluid spilling out. She had finally had her first taste of man flesh, and her friends and family collectively celebrated—she was no longer a child, but a woman. They came down upon him, taking turns to feed but leaving Lin to have her fill. They all remembered—there was nothing like your first.

Chapter Ten

Grosse Pointe Park, Michigan, USA
21st of November, 12:15 a.m. (GMT-5)

TThe late afternoon showers had passed through the Detroit suburb and left a cold blustery night in its place. The old oak tree in the front yard was denuded of its leaves, but the bare bones of its crown hinted at the majesty of the canopy in full bloom. The wooden sentinel swayed with an especially hard gust, tapping one of its branches against the window. Claire woke from her fitful dreams at the slight noise and stared out from behind the side rails of her toddler bed. The wind howled and the shadows danced, made more menacing in her imaginative eyes.

Claire shut her eyes hard and squeezed her teddy bear harder. She prided herself on being a very grown-up four-and-a-half-year-old, and she was going to try it mommy's way: close your eyes, count to ten, and see if the scary was still there when you opened your eyes. She could tell mommy didn't believe in monsters, and part of Claire wanted to be grown up like her, but she still counted to ten in the quietest whisper—if there were any monsters under her bed or in the closet, she didn't want them to know she was awake.

When her brown eyes cracked open in the smallest of peeks, she saw her room as it always was: her toy chest against the wall, her closed closet door opposite her bed, and a small set of furniture for her tea parties. Her heart was still racing despite the appearance of normality; things didn't feel right. She knew what would happen if she got out of bed and woke up mommy—there wouldn't be anything there and she would get in trouble. But then Claire remembered—mommy's friend was sleeping over. She'd believe her.

Claire summoned her courage and wiggled her way to the end of the bed where the side rail ended. The nightlight, which was usually comforting, created another set of shadows. Even though they were still, more shadows were no comfort to Claire. She hesitated for a moment; in the logic of her own making, once she got out of bed, her course was set and somehow more dangerous.

She held onto her teddy as her bare feet made contact with the cold floor. With the die cast, she hustled out of her room and crept down the hall to mommy's bedroom, noting each creak along the way. Everything seemed different at night in the dark. She put her ear on the door and listened. Mommy's soft snore rumbled on the other side. She put her little hand on the doorknob and turned it.

Joan Liu heard the soft patter of little feet on the hardwood floor long before she felt the small tug on her pajamas. She knew it couldn't be too serious if Claire wasn't crying or screaming, but didn't want to put her off. It was rare for Claire to go to her before her mother, and if it meant letting Allison sleep through the night, so be it.

"What is it, sweetie?" Liu whispered.

"I had a bad dream," Claire matched her volume.

Liu nodded, trying hard not to smile at the cherubic face that was so earnest. Claire's nightmares had improved once Joan had put up a ward against boogeymen and other nuisance creatures that liked to scare young children. They were generally harmless, and children eventually out-grew being affected by their mischief, but in her mind, maintaining a simple ward was a small price to pay for everyone to have a good night's sleep.

Liu grabbed her robe from the bedpost and slipped it on over her flannel pajamas. "I'll come check it out. We'll let mommy sleep."

Relief flooded the girl's face, and she wondered if all children felt things so intently or if Claire was just a particularly sensitive kid. Claire was already at the door waiting impatiently while Liu tightened her robe. At the last second, she slipped the switch knife she kept under the pillow into her pocket. It was balanced like any other blade, but the sigils inlaid with silver would be especially useful against the supernatural. It was probably nothing, but it never hurt to be prepared.

Liu gave Claire her left hand, and the determined girl regained her moxie now that she had reinforcements—if there were any bad things in her room, Aunt Jo would get rid of them. Liu stopped her at the door. "You'd better let me check things out first," she said seriously. Claire gravely nodded in agreement.

Liu summoned her will and swept the room. She found nothing but made a production of it. She ruffled the blankets and patted the bed down. She got on her hands and knees and checked underneath the low-clearance frame. She spun around quickly and made a sneak attack on the closet door, giving any lurking monsters no time to hide. Last, she rummaged through the toy chest. When Liu gave Claire the all clear, the little girl was satisfied with thoroughness of the search and re-entered her room, calm and reassured.

Claire asked her stay with her, just until she fell asleep. Liu's heart melted just a little at the request. She'd been seeing Allison for over a year, and Claire had taken her time in deciding whether or not she liked her mommy's new friend. Liu drew back the sheets and tucked Claire into bed before taking a position next to her on top of the covers for an easy escape once the girl drifted off. It was a tight squeeze on the toddler's bed, but Liu was petite—five-foot-four and slim. She lay down on her side and used her robe for cover.

"Can you tell me a story?" Claire asked in a sleepy voice.

"What kind of story?" Liu answered Claire with a question of her own.

Claire looked off into nothingness. "Something with a

princess. And she fights dragons. But she likes to wear pink."

The implied opposition amused Liu. Allison fought hard against enculturation of gender norms in their house, but some girls really do just want to wear pink. She began in a soft cadence, "Once upon a time, there was a princess who lived in big castle in a peaceful valley between two mountains."

"What's the princess's name?" Claire inquired as she turned on her side and held her bear fast. She wiggled herself backward until she was safely sandwiched between teddy and Aunt Jo.

"Funny you should ask," Liu feigned surprise, "but her name was also Claire." Claire smiled, and Liu didn't know if it was because she was in on the ruse or because the princess shared her name. "And Princess Claire loved to ride her horse and visit her subjects, to make sure everything was safe and good in her kingdom."

"What was her horse's name?" Claire yawned out.

"Pegasus," Liu answered. Claire settled down and her eyelids became heavy and dropped as Liu spun a yarn about a princess in pink riding her flying horse and slaying an evil dragon. By the end of the story, Claire's breathing became steady, deep, and slow with a slight snore—something she inherited from her mother.

Liu slowly untangled herself from Claire's side, trying her best not to wake her. She was almost out of bed when Claire rolled on her back. "Aunt Jo, wear your glasses," she mumbled, half-asleep, before rolling onto her other side. Liu paused at her words and waited for her to go back to sleep before attempting to move again. She quietly closed the door and softly stepped down the hall.

"Is Claire okay?" Allison muttered as Liu entered the room.

"Yeah, just a bad dream," she reassured her as she slipped off her robe and secretly slid the knife back under the pillow as she came back to bed. "I checked for monsters, told her a story, and snuck out once she was sound asleep."

Allison propped herself up on one elbow. "Look at you, nailing kid duty."

Liu cut eyes at her. "I can't tell if I'm being complimented, patronized, or made fun of."

"Why does it have to be just one?" Allison teased and playfully pulled her into an embrace. "I'm glad Claire trusts you, and if you're good with my kid, that makes you aces in my book."

Liu absentmindedly stroked Allison's long arms with her hand. "Does Claire talk in her sleep?"

"Sometimes, usually gibberish that I can't make out," Allison answered. "Why?"

"Claire told me to wear my glasses," Liu puzzled.

Allison raised an eyebrow. "But you don't wear glasses." She shrugged it off. "She was probably having a dream."

Liu put it aside but couldn't quite shake it off. She focused on the warm woman beside her. "I'm sorry I woke you up. I was hoping to take care of it and let you sleep."

"You didn't wake me up," Allison replied. "Your phone did." She reluctantly released Liu from her grasp so she could roll to her side and fish out her phone from the nightstand. There were only so many numbers that would buzz during this time of night, and Allison was one of them. Her demeanor stiffened as she read the message from the Salt Mine.

The silhouette of Liu's sleek form was backlit by the dim light from the screen, and Allison watched her partner's shoulders tense up. "Let me guess—it's work and you have to go," she predicted.

Liu tapped out a reply and set an early alarm on the phone before shut down the screen. "You're half right. I've got to swing by the office before an early flight out, but I can catch a few hours of sleep." She coaxed Allison over to her side of the bed.

"You work too hard," Allison observed, but cuddled up nonetheless.

Liu stroked her hair and kissed her head. "That's rich coming from a single mom running her own company."

"Stop talking to me. I'm trying to get some sleep here," she joked. They settled against each other and Allison quickly resumed her slumber. Joan Liu—codename Aurora—lay perfect still holding onto her paramour. Tomorrow, she was going out on a mission, and Liu never took for granted that each time could be the last time. She breathed her in and took solace in her touch until she dozed off herself.

*****

Sukchu Yi blew smoke rings from his pipe and contemplated his patch of the Newberry Campground. It had been a long and winding road that brought him from Korea to the Upper Peninsula of Michigan. He'd lost count of how many battles he'd fought in his many years, and he no longer cared to enumerate the scars left behind. For all the wrongs he'd tried to right, the universe did what it wanted anyway, because things were rarely as simple as singular cause and effect. There were aftershocks, ripples, and unintended consequences.

He'd no doubt that everything was unfolding as it should, as it had done before and would continue to do in the future, regardless of his personal feelings about how things hashed out. That was the nature of cosmic forces; they didn't much care how anyone felt about the matter or what name was ascribed to them—be it karma, fate, kismet, dharma—they just were. Once he'd come to terms with that, he took himself out of the game.

Here, he was Chuck, just another guy having a smoke under the extended canopy of his Airstream camper that doubled as a porch. Although it was very far from where he'd started, he was content to live out his days in peace and quiet in the UP. It had an ambience that reminded him of home even though it was someone else's homeland. His motherland had changed so much it hardly resembled what resided in his memory. If the world was hell bent on undoing itself, at least he would have a pretty view when it all crapped out.

He drew in another puff and considered the darkness that lay just beyond the beams of light from the periodic street lamps illuminating the RV park. Not all was right with the woods, and it wasn't just this business with chronic wasting disease. The trees were nervous and the waters unsettled. The animals were skittish—not just the deer and small creatures, but the bears and wolves too. When he cast his vision far and wide, there were things lurking in the shadows, evading his gaze. Even the manitous were on alert.

His policy of non-engagement had served him well over the years, but try as he might, he could not dismiss or ignore the signs. He'd already taken defensive measures and strengthened his personal wards, but a niggling notion pecked away at him and he had a decision to make—action or inaction. The idea of him girding for battle made him laugh. He was an old man, and his warrior days were long past. But there was more in his arsenal than swords, axes, and staffs…

When he did his mental accounting, Yi didn't count the ritual he'd performed earlier this summer as getting involved— that was doing a favor for an old friend. He hadn't *tried* to save the world, and if humanity hadn't been consumed en masse by an outsider as a byproduct of his actions, that was all right by him. If he were being completely honest, it'd felt good to throw around some big magic again.

It had been decades since he had a philosophical quandary, and he felt the press of things bigger than himself on his shoulders. He knocked out his spent bowl but declined to pack another. The smoke had given him clarity—he had been asking the wrong questions. The academic argument he'd been having in his head was a moot point if the universe had already decided to throw him into the thick of it.

Yi rose from his chair and went inside to grab the keys to his truck. The old but reliable engine started up after a little grousing, and he headed into town to retrieve his tools. He mused that part of him must have known this day would come, which was why he put his gear in storage instead of getting rid of it completely. He wasn't sure what the future held, but he knew two things. First, doing nothing was a choice and wouldn't absolve him from his share of responsibility for what followed. Second, there was no fool like an old fool.

He looked at himself in his rearview mirror and grinned like a teenager.

Chapter Eleven

Detroit, Michigan, USA
28th of October, 10:20 a.m. (GMT-4)

Joan Liu's home looked like a small tornado had touched down within its walls. Articles of clothing were haphazardly strewn over every available surface, there were empty glasses and half-drunken cups of tea scattered throughout the apartment, and the table in the dining room was mostly there to hold mail. Anyone else might have suspected it had been burgled, but Liu recognized the order in the chaos as her own as soon as she pulled her keys from the lock and shut the door behind her.

She deposited the unimportant mail atop its brethren and swept the lot into a box for recycling, stashed discreetly under the table. She corralled the dishes into the dishwasher and took a circuitous path to the bedroom, picking up all the clothes along the way and tossing them into the hamper. Then, she hastily pulled the comforter over her unmade bed and rummaged through her closet. It was a pre-mission ritual she had done many times, because even though she may have not been much of a domestic goddess, she loathed the thought of someone coming in and finding her place in such a state. She could hear her mother's rebukes in her head: I didn't raise you in barn; what will people think!

It took ten minutes to put an orderly veneer over her messy abode before she turned her attention to packing. With her special issue Salt Mine luggage open wide, Liu threw in her clothes, toiletries, and other personal items in the main compartments before opening the secret one. With a decisive sweep of her arm, she pushed all the clothes and jackets aside, isolating her extensive shoe racks. While Liu did have a weak spot for footwear of all types, it was also a handy way to hide her blades in plain sight with the help of a little glamour spell. She reached behind the columns and unhooked the latch, releasing a bandolier of knives, each balanced for throwing despite the magical silver sigils etched in the steel. She pulled two of her favorite hand-to-hand blades from behind her black knee-high boots, and from the false back of her teakwood chest, she pulled out a passport and a stack of cash. She did a quick check on sigils, edges, and tips before carefully packing them away in the secret compartment of her luggage. While she was less than fastidious with her housework, she was meticulous about what really mattered.

She put her walk-in closet back in order and dressed for travel—layers to accommodate a wide range of temperatures, slip-on shoes, and no belts or jewelry to take off for the TSA. She loaded her luggage into her car and raced to Zug Island to pick up her payload. Even though she had hours before her flight, getting caught in downtown morning rush hour traffic could easily derail her plans. There weren't many flights from Detroit to Houghton County Memorial Airport, and if she missed her plane, she was looking at a nine-hour drive.

The night guard was still on duty when she flashed her Discretion Minerals ID. "Good morning, Ms. Liu," he greeted her.

"Maybe for you. You're going home soon. I'm just starting a long day," she replied dryly. He smiled and handed her back her badge. Once the gate arm raised, she pulled her car into the underground parking lot and began the security song and dance that was entering the Salt Mine.

Technically, Joan Liu had two offices, one in the floors above ground as the environmental advisor for Discretion Minerals, and one below ground as Aurora, agent of the Salt Mine. Her background was in chemical engineering, and she first met Leader at a job fair as Angelica Zervo, CEO of Discretion Minerals. The prospect of working at a company run by an experienced female CEO had appealed to Liu after putting in a few years at an oil and gas company that existed for executive bonuses and was run by incompetent nepotistic old frat boys who held cigar and brandy meetings at gentlemen's clubs.

She didn't know how Leader knew about her abilities, but a few months into the job, Liu was approached for an entirely different promotion. After training, Aurora was born, and she received her titanium key and a fifth-floor office in the Salt Mine.

Liu presented her palm at her office door, and a package was waiting for her on the desk. She opened the box and checked the items against the inventory: banishment bullets covering Southeast Asia, a tracking compass, a grounded canteen, and two pairs of glamour-biased sunglasses.

"Crap," she muttered as she remembered Claire's words from last night. There were a few surefire ways to kill a relationship, and she was pretty sure telling your girlfriend that her daughter may be prescient was one of them. Liu checked the time and kept moving. The bullets were the only thing she had to conceal from security scanning; everything else could hide in plain sight.

She parked in long-term parking at the airport, uncertain how long she would be this time. As a general rule, LaSalle never booked her a return flight. Liu was an enforcer, called in when a certain level of precision and martial prowess was required. If Liu did her job right, all the bodies would be back in their native planes and out of the mortal realm. Her preferred weapons were edged, and although she did know how to shoot a gun, she knew the bullets were for Martinez.

As a seasoned traveler, Liu was intimately familiar with Detroit Metropolitan Airport. Leader had sent her all over the globe as an assassin of the supernatural, and she often flew under the radar of standard security checks due to her petite frame. No one suspected the little Asian woman of packing banishment blades.

As soon as she checked into her flight, she pulled up her phone and caught up on the brief, which was woefully thin. She flipped through the pictures of the four confirmed dead, the magical signatures found at the locations, and the information Martinez had reported last night. Twelve against two—they weren't great odds, but she had been in worse predicaments. At least they would be able to track them with the compass.

Chloe and Dot had narrowed down the signature to Southeast Asia, which was a problem in and of itself. The Salt Mine's database of salt-casted signatures in that region was spotty at best. Armed with a description from the manitou, the twins had combed through the stacks for a matching description, but hadn't had much luck. The number of creatures in the Asian sphere that could be described as man-eating creatures with razor claws and sharp fangs that were vaguely feline in appearance was frankly alarming.

While they couldn't narrow it down to a specific creature, the theme of glamour kept recurring. They often disguised themselves as beautiful young women, masking their true nature until it was too late for their prey—thus, the sunglasses. Liu was fuzzy on the mechanics, but Weber had found a way for the wearer to see through illusion magic. They were ineffective against actual shape shifters and fae, who bent light to become invisible, but they also didn't weaken the barrier between realms like the more useful hag stone. Liu had used them before hunting down a lamia, and they'd proved quite effective. The only downfall was the *killer* headache you got when they worked a little too well: the more discrepancy between reality and illusion, the more it hurt one's brain processing it.

Liu's mission was stated clearly: whatever they were, banish them out of North America and visit the UP Magh Meall to figure out how they got here in the first place. That was what the canteen was for.

Eating and drinking in the middle lands was forbidden, mostly because mortals were not meant to feast upon the sustenance of the fae. That was why agents loaded up on food and drink before they left and often brought back-up food for when they returned, thirsty and famished if it had been some time.

Subsequently, traveling long distances in the Magh Meall was ill advised, and agents got as close to the location in the mortal realm as possible before crossing over. While people could go without food for weeks, when it came to water, it was only days. On the rare occasions that longer stints might be required, Chloe and Dot created the grounded canteen. Made of metal, the entire internal layer of aluminum was inscribed with runes. Theoretically, any water brought from the mortal realm in the canteen would remain safe for consumption in the Magh Meall, because the magic anchored the contents of the canteen in mortality. The librarians asserted that it was for emergency use only, and Liu noted the qualifier and smirked. *Emergency use? That's just another day at the office.*

Liu shot off a text to Martinez, letting her know her ETA in Houghton. As far as the people of Keweenaw Bay Indian Community were concerned, she was Janet Lee, the photographer for the article Tracy Martin was writing for the Institute of Tradition. Her phone buzzed with Martinez's reply: *Just in time for ladies day at the casino. Meet you at the airport.* Liu let out a terse laugh and put her phone away once the chirpy voice over the loud speaker announced boarding for first class passengers.

Chapter Twelve

East of McMillian, Michigan, USA
21st of November, 3:15 p.m. (GMT-5)

Liu pulled the seat belt loose and shifted her weight to the other butt cheek. Martinez was behind the wheel, steering the Jeep Cherokee Trailhawk down the state highway while Liu kept her eye on the compass for movement. Martinez had ground down the tooth and inserted it into the back panel of the compass, and they were just waiting for it to get into range. Until then, they occupied their minds with less serious pursuits—Marry, Fuck, Kill.

"Wonder Woman, Black Widow, Jean Grey," Martinez posited as the concrete passed steadily under her wheels.

Liu squinted. "So that's before Dark Phoenix?"

"Yeah, but you don't know that's coming," Martinez defined the parameters more precisely.

"I'd marry Wonder Woman—that one's a no brainer," Liu started. "She comes with her own invisible jet and she's into bondage, although I could live without the lasso of truth. But it's a tough call between the other two," she hemmed and hawed. "They would both be great in the bed for different reasons, but I'm going to have to kill Jean Grey and fuck Black Widow."

Martinez looked askance in the general direction of the passenger seat. "You'd rather keep a trained assassin around instead of a psychic?" she puzzled.

"The worst Black Widow could do is kill me. Jean Grey is telepathic and telekinetic. Even if I didn't know she was going to turn into Dark Phoenix, that's a much higher risk to keep her around after a hook up, not just for me but for everyone," Liu explained her rationale.

"So you're fucking Black Widow for the good of the world—" Martinez clarified.

"Not all heroes wear capes," Liu retorted. She caught movement out of the corner of her eye and looked down to confirm the compass needle had popped to life. "We've got signal!" she announced. "Your hunch was right—keep bearing east."

Liu pushed away the food wrappers from lunch and unearthed the map of the area. While the needle sought the magical source as the crow flies, they had to use the roads as much as possible, which meant they were basically playing the longest game of vehicular "Hot or Cold" ever. When the needle took an abrupt swing, they'd gone too far along that road. Liu navigated and kept track of their current location on the map, letting Martinez know which way to turn when she doubled back. Sadly, she would have to wait to find out which

Hemsworth brother Martinez would off.

After a few minutes, they passed Newberry Country Club and headed south down a county road. As the streets got smaller and more remote, the pavement turned to gravel. Liu switched to the satellite images on her phone once they were really in the boonies.

The compass point did an abrupt turn after Martinez passed a long driveway on the right. "That's our location," Liu said emphatically and checked her phone. "Satellite shows a single structure on the lot. Looks like a house, I think."

"Find me a place to pull over so we can approach on foot," Martinez requested. "I don't want to lose the element of surprise by pulling into the driveway."

They pulled off the main road and found an inconspicuous place to park the SUV. Martinez opened the back, and they geared up. She loaded her Glock and pocketed another magazine with Southeast Asian banishment bullets, which gave her twelve shots total. She had one more magazine packed with North American bullets, just in case they were in cahoots with an evil manitou. She secured her carbon knife on her hip holster and brought binoculars with night vision capability—she'd prepared to encounter their quarry in the dark, but was relieved to get a bead on the pack well before sundown.

Liu slung her bandolier across her chest and strapped her larger blades on each thigh. All told, she had thirteen knives on her person, twelve of them enchanted for banishment. She passed Martinez a pair of glamour-biased sunglasses. "We're on a mission from Gaad," she quoted in a thick Chicago accent.

"Let's get the band back together on their own turf," Martinez replied, slipping on the shades that were so old, they had gone out and come back into fashion. Even though it was hunting season, they left the orange clothing in the car. Martinez reasoned that any hunter that strayed too close was already dead and hardly posed a threat compared to what they were stalking.

Their approach was nigh noiseless. While Martinez had her moccasins to thank for her silence, Liu moved with preternatural stealth. They found the structure was actually a small cabin, and unlike the satellite image, there was a compact car parked in front with Michigan license plates. Liu signaled to Martinez that she was going to do a perimeter sweep while Martinez parked herself in the woods and ran the plates. The seven-year-old Ford Focus was registered to Jacob Reeves with a permanent address in Detroit. She ran the name along with the address of the cabin by the Salt Mine to see if there were any hits.

While she waited, she zoomed in the binoculars on the windows, looking for signs of movement. Unfortunately, the curtains were drawn and there was no light source within to cast shadows against the late afternoon sun. Martinez gathered her will—*Hail Mary, full of grace*—and grabbed the large bead of the rosary in her pocket. The magical focus that Weber gifted her provided the extra oomph she needed to cover the distance from the tree line. She probed the cabin but found no wards, alarms, or resistance.

Liu returned and made a little noise to give Martinez some warning on her approach. "Front door is the only entrance," she reported in hushed tones. "There is a window on the west side but the blinds are closed. They're definitely inside. The compass needle was fixed on the cabin no matter which side I was on."

"Any wards?" Martinez whispered.

"Not that I picked up," Liu answered.

"Me neither," Martinez concurred and lowered her binoculars. "The car belongs to Jacob Reeves. I sent a request to the Salt Mine for more information. Is it possible that we are dealing with a magician that summoned them here?"

Liu considered it but quickly dismissed it. "If he brought them over, there would be no need for them to travel the Magh Meall. A summoning circle is a direct flight."

Martinez conceded the point. "There wasn't a flag on the car, so it doesn't look like Reeve is a missing person or wanted by law enforcement."

"Why don't I go in and ask him," Liu suggested.

"You want us to storm the castle?" Martinez asked incredulously.

"No, I want you to hang back and cover me while I go inside and take care of them," Liu corrected her.

Martinez felt a knot form in the pit of her stomach. If she were with Wilson, they would have waited for more information and done recon, probably *at least* overnight, before going in. If Hobgoblin were here, he would just blow things up from afar without putting either of them in much danger. But what Liu was suggesting sounded like a suicide mission. There was a reason Martinez called it in when she found out there were twelve supernatural creatures, and it wasn't to send someone else over the top.

Liu was touched by her reluctance but pressed the issue. "There's a reason Leader sent me to back you up. This is our one chance to catch them with their guard down, and we are losing light." She put her hand on Martinez's arm. "I've read the brief and know the odds. I've got this, especially if I have you covering my back."

Martinez swallowed her doubts and nodded in agreement. "Hold back until I'm inside and keep these on," Liu tapped the rim of her shades. Martinez watched Liu soundlessly disappear into the woods.

Liu returned to the eastern side of the cabin where there were no windows, and a series of trees and bushes to provide a modicum of cover en route to the cabin. She wound her will around her herself, forming a magical mantle that resembled a garland of flowers. It elevated her senses, reflexes, speed, stamina, and strength. By the time she broke through the brush, the magic was coursing through her fully.

Martinez watched Liu as she crept up to the cabin, crouching to pass underneath the windows at the front of the structure. She felt unwieldy with the large sunglasses on, but they had to stay on if she wanted to be able to distinguish reality from illusion.

With Liu well on her way, Martinez took a position behind Jacob Reeves's car, the gravel beneath her feet failing to crunch thanks to her moccasin-covered feet. Although small, the Ford Focus gave her some cover and a good vantage of the front door and the western window, in case anyone tried to bail in the fight. It was also within sprinting distance if it sounded like Liu was in trouble.

When Liu made it to the front door, her heightened senses heard snoring through the cracks in the frame and doorjamb. She reached for the knob and cast a spell to keep the mechanisms and hinges from squeaking—as the adage went, wake not a sleeping lion. She tested the door and it opened with ease.

Daylight flooded into the small, dark cabin, and Aurora lived up to her codename. It took Liu a spilt second to take in the remains of Jacob Reeves and the sleeping pile of fur with limbs, tails, and heads piled on top of each other for warmth and reassurance. Unfortunately, not everyone was taking a nap.

Liu couldn't be sure what form the creature was projecting, but she saw three bipedal humanoid tigers were standing in front of her. Their faces was almost human except for the vertical slit pupils of their predatory eyes and the sharp fangs in their maws. Their fur was bloodstained around the mouth and hands, which ended in sharp, claw-like fingernails. They exchanged glances and one stepped forward. "Can I help you?" the creature asked civilly in a decidedly feminine voice. The other two stepped toward Liu on either side—she recognized an attack formation when she saw one.

Liu sprang into motion and pulled two throwing knives in rapid succession. The ones on the left and straight ahead screeched when the blades found purchase and their bodies disappeared, banished back from whence they came. Liu's two knives hit the ground as their targets blinked out of the mortal realm and their yells were replaced by two resounding thuds. The third charged with a battle cry, claws extended.

It was closing in fast, and Liu bent backward and to the side to dodge the barbed swipe. She pulled out the hunting knife strapped to her left thigh and sliced cleanly across the neck of her attacker. It didn't have time to scream out in pain before vanishing from the mortal realm. A nick from a banishment blade was enough to send a supernatural creature back to its native realm, but Liu cut to kill whenever possible; most of the time a banishment strike was instantaneous, but on the very rare occasion it could take half a second or more.

The noise and commotion awoke the mound of fur, and bodies disentangled and scattered in different directions. Liu pulled out her other hunting knife and went to work. A pair came at her from either side. She dropped down and slid out of the flanking maneuver, slashing at their thighs as she passed. A spurt of arterial spray shot out before the pair dematerialized.

Another cluster came at her, trying to back her into a corner. She turned around and ran toward the wall, using the momentum to propel herself up and over the pack. They were fast, but she was faster. Once she was behind them, she made deep cuts along two backs and sliced another throat.

Of the four remaining, two broke ranks and ran for the front door, only to be met by Martinez's banishment bullets. The other two simultaneously leapt at Liu, and time slowed in her vision. She hurled a knife into one but the other landed on her hard, knocking her second knife out of her grip. Using both her arms, she kept the monster from pinning her down, and in her adrenaline-fueled and magically enhanced awareness, Liu heard Martinez's approach despite her magical footwear.

Liu guessed she had seconds before Martinez was in range to take a shot, and in that split second, she had to make a choice: banish the creature or get a piece of it before Martinez did. Liu bucked and elbowed the creature off her with a strength that surprised her attacker. Then she rolled out and grabbed its tail. With her other hand, she pulled the mundane knife strapped to her ankle and severed the end with a swift flick of the wrist. Howling in pain, it flailed its talon-like nails at Liu. All its focus was directed at the mortal that took its tail, and it failed to notice Martinez entering the cabin.

"Take the shot!" Liu yelled as she skittered backward,

holding onto the tail and holding the plain knife defensively.

Martinez fired again and hit it square between the shoulders, and the cabin abruptly turned quiet. "I got three," Martinez spoke.

"And nine makes twelve," Liu added, releasing the tail and catching her breath.

Martinez cleared the two rooms behind closed doors; one was a bathroom, the other a bedroom. "We're clear," she announced as she holstered her gun. Liu slid her sunglasses on top of her head and was giving herself a once over for injuries. "You okay?"

"I'm having a better day than them…or Jacob Reeves, for that matter," Liu replied, nudging her head toward the only remains in the building. The room was spattered in blood and whatever glamour was once in place was gone now. The corpse had been eviscerated and all the internal organs devoured. There were bite and claw marks on what little flesh remained, and it would have been difficult to identify the body except the face was largely untouched.

"He hasn't been dead too long by the smell of it," Martinez commented as she followed Liu's lead. She was just starting to get a hint of a headache and slipped the glasses over her head as well. She donned a pair of gloves from her pocket and fished out his keys, wallet, and phone from his overcoat. She mechanically rifled through his wallet and found his ID, bank card, credit cards, and cash. "Well, it's definitely Jacob

Reeves," she confirmed after matching the photo to the face. His phone's battery still had a charge but the screen was locked. She pulled a flash drive from her bag and made a duplicate of the phone's contents, which Weber had rigged to not require user authentication. "It doesn't make any sense. This guy is no hunter."

"Based on the knee pads and Velcro pants, I would say he's a stripper," Liu surmised. Martinez used the end of stick to lift up the shreds of his thong.

"So now they are having their food delivered?" Martinez asked rhetorically as she put everything back where she found them.

"Beats getting mauled by a spirit bear in the woods," Liu pointed out. "But it would suggest a higher level of familiarity with the mortal realm. Unless he was an unlucky schmo passing through, he was led here intentionally. I've hunted a lot of supernatural things and none of them knew enough about technology and currency to engage an exotic dancer." She started picking up her blades and wiping them down on the remains of Reeve's discarded clothing. Usually Liu was fastidious about forensic evidence, but since this was the scene of a magical murder, they were going to burn the place once they were done to cover their presence anyway.

"That's not the only weird thing. He's still got his eyes," Martinez replied. "All the other bodies were missing them. I suppose it could be a fluke because those were outside. Crows, ravens, and rodents all love a good juicy eyeball…" Neither of them was convinced by her theory, however. She pulled her saltcaster and checked Reeves for a magical signature. When the white grains remained still, she salted the rest of the cabin.

There were plenty of variations on the same pattern as before, but on the floor of the empty bedroom, Martinez picked up something new. She snapped a picture on her phone and kicked the magic out of the salt. The grains filled in cracks of the wooden flooring, and a faint arc across two different planks of wood caught her attention.

Martinez took out a sachet of salt and poured out a little more, revealing a small circle no more than six inches across. She distributed the pearly granules into the shallow ridges until she could get more detail on the unfamiliar characters. It resembled a summoning circle, but its curvature was more rustic; no one had pulled out a compass to scratch out a perfect circle. While Martinez didn't recognize the name, she did notice it lacked many of the usual caveats practitioners put around the circle for protection. Additionally, it was way too small for the cat creatures to stand inside. She snapped a few pictures before scattering the salt and blowing it out of the grooves. When Martinez returned to the main room, Liu was putting eight inches of severed tail into a plastic sack.

"Never figured you the sort to keep souvenirs," she ribbed Liu.

Liu grinned. "You never know when you might need a

piece of a critter, and Chloe and Dot may be able to use it."

"I found something in the bedroom—a circle with characters I don't recognize. They mean anything to you?" Martinez held up the phone to show Liu.

"Nope, but there isn't much to it," she remarked at the bare bones circle.

Martinez shook her head. "What the hell is going on?"

"No idea, but they aren't here anymore, so we've got that going for us," Liu drily remarked.

"Have you ever run across those things before?" Martinez inquired.

"Nope, but they were fast and ugly," Liu summed up.

"They were rakshasas," a grizzled voice came from the door. Liu and Martinez grabbed their weapons and whipped their sunglasses back on. When Liu saw the old Asian man at the door didn't change shape, she held back on the throwing knife in her hand.

"And who are you?" she demanded.

"It's okay," Martinez assured her, lowering her weapon as soon as she confirmed he was as he appeared. "This is Chuck, the UP's resident shaman and master fisherman. Chuck, meet Liu."

Chapter Thirteen

The Outer Lands
Summer Epoch

Faye plunged into nothingness and braced herself for impact. She didn't know where she would end up, but she figured the falling had to stop eventually because she was in too much pain to be dead. She landed on all fours, and a wave of agony radiated across her body from the piercing wound in her shoulder. The clean crisp smells suggested she was somewhere in the Magh Meall, and when she opened her eyes, the pale lavender tint to the light confirmed her suspicions.

As she took in more of her surroundings, she knew she was no longer in the Upper Peninsula. It was warm and humid rather than cold and brisk. All the trees had their leaves, not just the evergreens. The air was pregnant with the perfume of orchids, whose color and shape were as varied as their number. Even the faeries looked different. Faye was no longer in the land of sasquatch and manitou. She was home.

Every culture had a magical realm between the world of humans and the world of fantastic fae, but in the Asian sensibility, they were not called the middle lands. Culturally, being in the center was a place of primacy, and everything outside of the middle was by definition lesser and barbaric. This plane had many names, but they all translated to roughly the same: the Outer Lands.

The rakshasas had lived in the Outer Lands for ages, but it was not where they began their existence. They were breathed into life in heaven and promptly cast out when they fed on their creator. Faye never understood why they were created as the physical manifestation of hunger if they were not meant to feast. Even among the animals and mortals, were the young not nourished by their parents?

For a time, the rakshasas roamed the mortal realm, using their innate magical abilities to choose a less frightening form. Once humans discovered mass violence, they had a use for natural predators and welcomed them in their armies. The rakshasas had fought many epic wars under different banners, and it was a time of plenty for them. They slaked their thirst in the rivers of blood.

But when people no longer found use for their insatiable voracity, they cast them out as well. No matter who claimed the Middle Land—the gods in heaven or man in the mortal realm—the rakshasas were always on the outside.

"Faye, you're alive!" she heard a familiar voice crest the hill. Her heart lightened in the knowledge that she was not alone; another of her pack was with her. She felt a prickled tongue lick her wound clean before putting pressure on it to staunch the bleeding. "There's more coming, Faye. I'm going to need your help."

Faye rose and joined her as more rakshasas landed. They sorted them into two groups—those that could be saved and those who had already expired. Everyone was wounded, but the ones who were less so helped the more grievously injured. They dug out bullets with their claw-like digits, cleaned wounds with their saliva, and dressed them with the chewed mash of medicinal plants. Lin was the last to return, tail clipped and shot through the heart. The final tally was in—they had left the Outer Lands thirteen strong, and only seven had returned alive.

The survivors roiled with rage and sorrow. There were accusations thrown around. Old disagreements reemerged and found fertile soil in their indignant grief. The traditionalists believed they were being punished for straying from the old ways. The conservatives echoed their original concern with traveling to distant lands. The progressives saw the entire operation as an indictment of Popo and called for new leadership. Emotions ran raw and fierce; they knew no other way to be.

In the past, Popo had used aggression and dominance to restore order, but she suspected that a show of brute strength wasn't going to work this time. That tactic worked if *she* was the one that broke them, only because she could then put them back together again in a configuration more pleasing to her vision.

But the pack was already broken by a bad defeat. What they needed was comfort, and Popo positioned herself to provide accordingly. She growled at a low frequency, one that was felt more than heard. Tired and ragged, the pack simmered down. "Now is not a time for bickering. We have lost many a fierce huntress, including our dear Lin." Popo evoked the youngest of them, appealing to their tender side and the sadness of a life cut too soon in its development. "Casting blame will not bring them back. Let use mourn our dead, lick our wounds, and find respite in the pack."

Popo circled the bodies of the fallen and sang a doleful elegy in their native language. Their hearts ached as she extolled the virtues and recounted the deeds of each rakshasi, and one by one, the pack fell into line and joined her. When Popo finished her requiem, they all bid a final farewell to their fallen before biting into the corpses. They tore meat from bone and swallowed pieces of their dead with tear-stained faces—may their flesh feed the strength of the pack.

When the ritual observance was done, they curling up together to sleep through the night, seeking the solace and warmth of the group. Despite their personal differences of opinions, all wanted to be soothed tonight. Popo eased her way into the center of the heap, and the rakshasas shifted to afford her a place in the middle.

Sleep eluded Faye. Her mind was restless, unwilling to forgive or forget. Others might be lulled by custom and honeyed entreaties to return to the status quo, but not Faye. She'd had her doubts about Popo's latest scheme to expand their hunting grounds, but she'd kept her opinions to herself. It was never wise to be too free with your mind when it came to Popo.

Were Faye in charge, she would have shifted the pack in a different direction all together. She didn't want to hunt men down in the forests, and doing it in exotic locales didn't make it any more attractive. The cities were full of food, and there were new ways to hunt and eat in the urban jungle. The mortal realm had moved on since their expulsion; why shouldn't they?

She'd tried to work within the existing power structure and was even hopeful when they'd allowed her to arrange Lin's initiation using her newfangled technology. There had been no complaints when a beautiful man appeared at their front door—clean, hair-free, muscled, and oiled up—but the near proximity to the tragedy was enough to taint and scuttle any progress she'd made. They would recoil at future attempts to modernize, and it wasn't just the traditionalists. They were closing ranks, and there was no place for nuance and causality when it came to herd thinking. Faye didn't need a proclamation to know which way the wind was blowing; the pack spoke through its actions. Why else was she on the outside of the sleep huddle instead of nearer the middle?

Faye had been regaled with stories of their past glories, and she wondered when they had stopped thinking of themselves as hunters and became minded like prey. She had been patient and paid her dues, and it had gotten her nowhere. She knew she could not challenge Popo and win, but perhaps she could strike her own deal. Once she established a viable alternative, how many rakshasas would be content with the old ways?

She listened to the soft purrs and the slow rhythmic pace of the pile's breathing—the pack was asleep. Faye untangled herself from the arms, legs, and tails and snuck off into the night.

Chapter Fourteen

Newberry, Michigan, USA
21st of November, 4:45 p.m. (GMT-5)

"Wait, they eat their dead?" Martinez asked incredulously and put down her cup on the Formica tabletop of the Airstream's dining nook.

Sukchu Yi smiled obliquely—of all things he'd told her about the rakshasas, that was the one she found unbelievable. "Meat is nourishment and if they don't eat it, someone else will."

Liu turned pensive. "I can sort of see it. If someone has to eat me, I would want it to be my friends instead of my enemies." Martinez gave her an ambivalent head bob.

"It's a way to honor their dead and reinforce their social bonds while also refueling," Yi explained. "Rakshasas are always hungry, but never more so than after shedding blood."

"And that's how we could find them using the tooth of the one killed by the noozhe-makwa manidoo," Martinez started connecting the dots. "They ate her, and we were really following her remains in them."

"That, or they took her body to the cabin and consumed it

there," he replied.

Liu unconsciously raised her hand before posing her question, and it amused Yi to no end. It had been a long time since he was anyone's teacher. "If the rakshasas were banned ages ago, how did they re-enter the mortal realm?" she asked.

Yi nodded seriously. "That is a worrisome question."

"Perhaps they found a way to bypass the wards," Martinez threw out the suggestion.

"Or the wards have weakened over time," Liu posited. "Don't these kind of things need constant maintenance?"

"Generally, but there are ways to make spells more permanent," Yi answered cryptically.

"Is it possible that the magic keeping them out is only good for places that connect to their Outer Lands?" Martinez hypothesized. "Maybe that's why they traveled to the UP's Magh Meall before coming over." The theory garnered nods all around.

"But that still doesn't explain how they traveled through different middle lands," Liu pointed out. "And—no offense—why the Upper Peninsula?"

Martinez's pocket started buzzing, and it took some maneuvering to get her phone out in the cramped quarters. She'd sent off the new signature and the strange circle to the Mine for identification before torching the cabin, but her hopes of a rapid turnaround on those were dashed once she opened the communication.

"We've got an update," she said obliquely to Liu, whose phone went off as if on cue. Neither was sure what to make of Chuck. They knew he was a practitioner of some power, as evidenced by the fact that he had performed the ritual to stop the Hollow from consuming the mortal realm earlier this summer. He had been forthcoming with what he knew about rakshasas, and the wards on his camper were no slouch. Despite that, they'd agreed on the drive over to stick to protocol and keep a tight lid on Salt Mine sensitive information.

As they turned their attention to their screens, Yi gave them some privacy and rose to make more tea. He'd picked up on their vibe and made a tacit agreement: mutual assistance without asking too many questions. He couldn't remember the last time he had guests in his camper, and despite the gravity of rakshasas in the Upper Peninsula, he found himself enjoying the scene that was developing. He was accustomed to solitude, and the vibrancy of youth coupled with the challenge of unraveling a dilemma was a jolt of excitement in the otherwise mundane passage of time.

Chloe and Dot, the Salt Mine's librarians and font of all knowledge when it came to magic, had sent them what they had on rakshasas while they worked on the other unknown parts. Martinez glossed over the portions she had already ascertained through combat, observation, and talking to Chuck. Rakshasas were hungry maneaters that could wield magic as supernatural beings. Like all practitioners of the arts, there were things they could do and not do without any apparent rhyme or reason. In legend, they were known for illusion magic and renowned for their strength and martial prowess. The rakshasas fought in more than one of the Asian epics.

"It says here there are more than one kind of rakshasa because they exist in multiple pantheons: Hinduism, Buddhism, and Jainism. As those faiths spread, local cultures integrated them into their understanding of the cosmos," Martinez spoke without looking up from her screen.

Yi affirmed her statement. "Once upon a time, they were endemic to all of South and Southeast Asia. They entered Korea with Buddhism, but they also edged in anywhere Hinduism spread. Once the warlords were done using them as shock troops, they were let loose on the countryside." A darkness settled over the fine wrinkles in his face, giving them enhanced depth and age. When he noticed the intensity of stares his guests were giving him, he banished the gloom that hung over him. "Then, the magicians banded together and expelled them," he concluded and poured them newly steeped tea.

"Are they actually different creatures that have been erroneously given the same name or are they the same species with the capacity to change their behavior, like humans?" Martinez wondered aloud.

"A moot point when they're killing and eating people," Liu pointed out as she sipped her refreshed cup of perfectly steeped tea.

Martinez nibbled at one of the cookies he had set out on a dish while she mulled a niggling notion. She was less concerned about the classification mechanism as she was about the variation. "Regardless of how, if there are different kinds, theoretically, there could be good rakshasas too, right?" She looked up at Yi for confirmation.

"It is a possibility," Yi conceded. "Although telling the difference between a good one and a bad one may take more time than it takes for one to kill you. Rakshasas are intelligent creatures, capable of deceit, cunning, and strategy: all of them will *say* they're good."

"But if we could find a real good one, maybe they could help us figure out what the evil ones are up to," Martinez persisted on her train of thought.

"Says here Jain rakshasas are vegetarian," Liu commented laterally. She put her phone down and tilted her head sideways. "At least they have a reason why they are always hungry." Her stomach rumbled, and she fed it another cookie.

Martinez tapped out a quick message: *any good/non-evil rakshasas we could summon for information or help?* It seemed counterintuitive, but maybe the answer to a rakshasa problem was more rakshasas. She looked at the time on the upper corner of the phone and nudged Liu. "We should be getting back."

"Wouldn't want to miss ladies' night," Liu said sardonically as she put away her phone.

Martinez shuddered at the suggestion. The tea had helped

push her headache back, but it threatened to return at just the thought of ringing slot machines.

"How about a burger and beer?" Martinez counteroffered.

"You're my kind of lady," Liu stated for the record, then finished her tea and grabbed a cookie for the road. "Thank you for the refreshments and letting us lie low until the fire was out," she addressed Yi with a slight bow of the head.

"Thank you for sending the rakshasas home," he responded and bowed his head in kind. *As if Penny would ever forgive me if I let two of hers get picked up for murder and arson.*

"Won't be a permanent solution if we can't figure some things out," Martinez griped to mostly herself. She pulled out a card with just a phone number printed on it and held it out to Yi. "Chuck, if you come up with anything, will you give me call?"

He saw her earnest aura and the determination in her large brown eyes and knew he could not refuse. "Of course," he replied and pocketed the card.

He followed them outside and escorted them to their vehicle. Such chivalric gestures might have annoyed Martinez under different circumstances, but she gave Yi a pass in part because of his age. It felt oddly paternal, even though he barely knew them. As they climbed inside, he bid them well wishes. "May you have safe travels wherever this road takes you."

Martinez smirked at the implication in his words. "You as well."

Yi watched the Jeep Cherokee Trailhawk set out of the Newberry Campground and reciprocated as the two women waved at him through their back window as they got back onto the highway. He went inside, opened a can of soup into a pot, and set it on the stovetop. The microwave would have been faster, but this way tasted better, and tinned soup needed all the help it could get. He wasn't very hungry, but he knew he should eat something before embarking any further on the path he'd found himself.

He replayed the afternoon while he waited for the soup to simmer. It had been centuries since he'd seen a rakshasa. When a pair had burst through the front door of the cabin, he could hardly believe his eyes. He grasped at strands of memory that he'd long since put away, thinking those days were behind him. The distant past came rushing back, and with it, a fair amount of chagrin at the hubris and sense of invincibility he'd had then. *Youth is truly wasted on the young.*

The lid on the pot jostled as the steam escaped and broke his reverie. He took another look at the card Martinez had left him. *This is why I don't mix in*, he chided himself as he turned off the heat and grabbed the handle with a kitchen towel. He emptied the contents into a clean bowl and took it to the table. The noodles were too soft, the broth a little salty, and there was never enough vegetables for his liking, but he ate every drop plus a handful of crackers. He liked saltines for their positive blandness.

After he had cleared the table and washed up the dishes, he unhinged one of the many storage compartments of his camper; keeping one's clutter out of sight was integral to RV life. He pulled out the duffle bag he'd retrieved from storage last night and laid out the accoutrements of his past life on the bed.

He fanned out the layers of fabric, each a different color. The first robe he'd ever donned was white for purity, when he was chosen by the spirits to become a shaman. They had not been subtle, causing all sorts of maladies until he surrendered to the calling. He couldn't eat or sleep, and his body and soul ached until he allowed the divine wind to enter him. Since the day of his *naerim-gut*, Sukchu Yi had been a shaman, intercessor between the mundane and spirit world.

As a shaman, Yi wore all five colors through the course of a *gut*. Every rite started in white robes, as ritual cleansing was essential for any communion with the spiritual realm. Then he would put on red robes to invite interaction with the spirits while protecting against demons and evil ghosts. There were yellow robes for rebirth and rejuvenation, and black for wisdom—not just in understanding, but application of what the gods told him. Each ritual ended in blue robes for vitality and good luck; he used to joke that Korean shamans had more costume changes than Chinese brides.

He smiled softly at the recollection of twelve *gori guts*. They were heady communal affairs, full of music, singing, dancing, and storytelling, with equal parts dramatic reenactments and comedic relief. There was food and drink aplenty; it was a day of bounty and feast for man and gods alike. As he grew in spirit, he found he needed fewer accessories to communicate with the spirit world, but he went full regalia as long as he was serving communities. It helped orient people in the ritual. When he'd fled his homeland, he'd been forced to pare down to his essential focuses: a white fan, a bundle of brass bells, a small gong with a padded mallet, and a sheathed ceremonial dagger, all wrapped in a set of robes.

Tonight would be a more subdued ritual, and there wasn't enough room to conduct it in the two hundred square feet of his Airstream. He needed a safe place to perform it, somewhere he could work without being disturbed. He loaded his things into his truck and drove south to a quiet place near Pullup Lake. Hunting hours ended twenty minutes ago, but he wore an orange vest while he set up the site, just in case.

He picked a clearing close to the water that was known to him, and stacked dried wood for a central fire. He set a fire bundle underneath, coaxing the embers with his will and his breath. Once the flames were roaring, he donned his white robes and purified himself, repeating the prayers he'd said a million times before. He sprinkled water on himself and the fire, ritualistically cleaning the site. The flame hissed but did not falter. Next, he threw a precisely folded piece of white paper into the fire, symbolically purifying his body. He sang while he watched the flames consume it; the burnt flecks floated on an updraft into the darkening sky.

Yi modulated his song and opened his folded white silk fan with a flick of his wrist. The next gori began with beseeching the protective spirits to watch over this gut. He dragged his foot as he walked around the fire counter-clockwise and fanned inward, metaphorically reinforcing that whatever appeared inside the circle should stay within its bounds. Once the circle was complete, he changed to his red robes and struck the gong twelve times, marking the next gori.

Yi called out in ecstatic verse and invoked Sugala, using all her epithets: bearer of knowledge, most beneficent of the vidyadhara, walker of the righteous path, and cherished follower of tirthankara. He knew his voice and will would find their way, but he was uncertain if she would answer. Their history was complicated, the result of each of them following their own code to inevitable but ultimately dissatisfying results.

He could have forced her to make an appearance with a compulsive summoning, but he'd quickly dismissed such heavy-handed tactics. If such measures were needed for them to have a simple conversation, he was unlikely to get any useful help from her in the first place. In his mind, it was better to call and coax her arrival rather than try to force her compliance. That said, he still put a protective circle between himself and the fire, just in case Sugala had gone bad. Approaching in good faith was not mutually exclusive with letting one's guard down completely, especially when it came to inviting a rakshasi to him.

With the brand of persistence that stubborn old men could muster, he jostled the cluster of bells in one hand, determined to make quite a racket until Sugala replied, even if it was only to tell him to stop. Eventually a sharp wind bent the flames, and Yi was no longer alone.

Yi ceased his noisemaking and his gaze fell on a familiar face. She was as majestic as he remembered. Her sleek, lean form was covered in red fur with black strips, and her tail curled up at the tip. Her ears were pert, and her red eyes zeroed in on his voice. She had a hunter's biology, even though she'd long ago chosen the path of nonviolence. She spied the bounds of the circle and tested her will against them—enough to make it hard to cross, but not impossible. She wondered what he would have done if she had gone feral.

Sugala stayed well behind the line and addressed him. When she spoke, it rolled out like a melodic purr. "I see the years have not improved your voice or your face."

"And yet they have not faded your beauty," he replied graciously.

Amusement crept across her face. "Flattery? You must be desperate for my help," she remarked and swished her tail side to side.

Yi demeanor grew serious all at once. "Rakshasas have returned and started hunting men again."

"That's impossible," she cried in disbelief.

"I saw two with my own eyes, and it is said they were part of a pack of thirteen," he avowed.

"But the wards have held, even after all this time," Sugala objected. She need not state the obvious: if they wards had failed, her clan would not still be in the Outer Lands.

"Then someone is either summoning them or helping them cross over," Yi concluded for her benefit. "Do you know anything that could help?"

Her expression soured. "The last time I helped you, my entire clan was banished from their home and exiled into the Outer Lands."

Yi flinched as her words struck him, because they were true. His first instinct was to abnegate responsibility for how things played out. He wanted to tell her he'd protested the decision and was summarily shut down, that the community of practitioners felt an absolute ban was the only way to ensure the safety of all their communities. But he bit his tongue and swallowed the discomfort. That was the price of compromising his values and betraying his allies for what was sold as the greater good.

Cowed, he solemnly answered with a deep bow, "That was never my intention. *Yongseohaseyo*."

Sugala weighed his words and apology and found them acceptable. "Some martial clans have been recruiting. One of my ascetics was approached in the forest. They are promising renewed access to hunting the mortal realm," she informed him.

"How long ago was this?" he asked.

She had to think about it. Time passed different in the Outer Lands, and it had been a long time since she experienced time as mortals did. "Maybe three or four moons ago?"

He gently pressed for more information, "Do you know how they are coming over?"

Sugala shook her head. "There are rumors of an alliance with an old demon that predates even myself, but I don't have a name or the means."

"Do you have any idea of their strength?" he probed.

She smirked. "I don't consort with that branch of rakshasas for obvious reasons." Yi nodded in understanding—reformed rakshasas who voluntarily abstained from eating flesh had acquired a distasteful reputation among their kind. "But I know the offer is tempting. There are many who have only heard tales of the grand old days, and they are keen to see the mortal realm for themselves and taste the flesh of men. None of mine have broken their oaths, but I have heard that some of the daughters of Bakasura have returned to their savage ways."

"Thank you for answering my call and granting me your insight, Sugala," he said reverently and bowed deeply.

"*Haenguneul bileoyo, olaen chingu*," she answered in his native tongue before walking toward the fire and returning to the Outer Lands.

Chapter Fifteen

Baraga, Michigan, USA
21st of November, 8:30 p.m. (GMT-5)

Martinez and Liu lounged on the couch of their suite at the Ojibwa Casino. The TV was on, but they were only half watching in their slightly tipsy, postprandial haze. Liu was checking in with Allison; Claire had gotten in a fight at preschool. As a mother, she was mortified that her child had resorted to violence instead of using her words. As a feminist, she was proud that her daughter stood up to a little boy who had tried to bully her out of her toy. Martinez's phone buzzed in rapid succession, each one accompanied by appraising nods and the occasional eye roll.

"Who's blowing up your phone?" Liu salaciously inquired as she signed off with Allison.

"Don't get too excited," Martinez advised. "It's just Aaron. He's been shooting me ideas for Thanksgiving dinner. Based on some of his suggestions, I have the feeling he's been drinking wine while surfing the web."

"Ooohhh, lay them on me," Liu blithely chattered; she loved tragedy in all its forms.

"Well, here's his idea for a signature drink," Martinez zoomed in on the picture of a clear russet cocktail garnished an orange slice. "Cranberry milk punch. It's a colonial favorite," she added, tongue in cheek.

"You don't say?" Liu leaned in and furrowed her brow. "There's milk in that?"

"No, it's washed in milk. All the bitter crap in the tea and stewed cranberries causes the milk to curdle and gets trapped in the chunks so when you strain it through a cheese cloth, the punch is smooth and velvety," Martinez explained.

"So it's like an early Jägerbomb," Liu posited.

"A lot lower caffeine and alcohol content, but yes," Martinez agreed. "It's actually not a bad idea. It can be made days ahead of time and then you add the bubbly day of, or seltzer water for non-drinkers."

"Gotta have something to counter the tryptophan," Liu said drily. "What's that?" She pointed to another link.

"Oh, that's a blog post about five alternatives to green bean casserole," Martinez replied. "The dishes themselves aren't bad, but you have to scroll all the way to the end before it actually gives you the recipe. The author talks about her favorite Thanksgiving dinners before discussing the actual cooking in painful detail with tons of extraneous pictures along way."

Liu scanned the page and started reading aloud, "One warm November in the early 2000s, I found myself in Guatemala for Thanksgiving, far from home with nary a can of mushroom soup in sight." She stopped herself from continuing. "I see what you mean." Her gaze wandered to another link preview. "How to fold napkins?"

Martinez laughed at the mockery in her tone. "You haven't seen the playlist he's putting together for background music," she smirked.

"No!" Liu exclaimed. "A signature cocktail, fancy napkins, and its own soundtrack?"

"You're more than welcome to stop by if you find yourself scrounging your apartment for a can opener on Turkey Day," Martinez offered.

"I think it's cute that you think I own cans of soup, much less a can opener," Liu responded. She didn't spend much time in the kitchen and had more takeout numbers programmed into her contact list than she cared to admit. "Allison cooks a big meal and opens her doors to all her friends and any of their acquaintances that don't have anywhere else to be on Thanksgiving. I promised I would help out if I was in town."

"Things are still good on that front?" Martinez fished for as much information as Liu wanted to provide.

"Yeah. She doesn't ask too many questions, I don't make too many demands, and we enjoy the time we spend together," Liu said simply. "What about you and Aaron? You two are pretty adorable planning a holiday dinner party together, and he's cute, for someone with a penis."

"We like to play house, not doctor," Martinez remarked.

She kept quiet about Stigma and Fulcrum. If Liu didn't already know, it wasn't her place to inform her. "Plus, isn't there something against fraternizing with coworkers?"

Liu lightly shoved her shoulder. "Shut up. You're kidding, right?"

"I just assumed," Martinez said defensively. "I had a lot of other things to process when I was on-boarded."

"Right, magic's real, meet the resident devil, and be sure to fill out your time card on time…" Liu joked. "We're black op agents living—at minimum—double lives. It's not like we are going to get written up by HR for screwing around."

Martinez had spent the past year playing catch up in her new job, and she hadn't considered how difficult it must be to find and recruit Salt Mine agents in the first place. "And Leader doesn't give you a hard time having a significant other?" There wasn't a question in either of their minds that Leader knew about Allison. Leader seemed to know everything.

Liu gave it some thought before answering. "I have no doubt that she would prefer that I didn't—it's less messy for her that way—but it's never been mentioned nor alluded to," she replied diplomatically and shrugged. "As long as it doesn't interfere with getting the job done and you know how to keep a secret, it is what it is."

"I guess that makes sense," Martinez conceded. "There's no way Hobgoblin or Deacon are keeping it in their pants, but hooking up isn't the same thing as being in a relationship. Were there any married Salt Mine agents?"

"If there were, I would think everyone would keep quiet about it," Liu conjectured. "But I doubt that it's been common. The nature of the job is usually enough to put an expiration date on most relationships: the long hours when you're on a case, the traveling—often at the last minute—and all the things you can't share with them. Even if you decide to tell your partner you work for the FBI or the CIA, you're not telling the whole truth. Someone you're intimate with will pick up on that eventually, and if they don't, you're not really that close with them, which carries its own problems."

"That's a lot of wise insight for someone who decided to order another round of margaritas 'because it's ladies' night,'" Martinez lightened the mood with a little good-natured ribbing.

"I've been sabotaging my own relationships long before Leader came into my life," Liu boasted grandly in a self-depreciating manner.

Martinez's phone rang in earnest, and the caller ID indicated it was a redirected call. "Hello?" she answered without giving her name.

"This is Chuck. I'm calling for Teresa," the raspy voice said over the line.

"Oh, hi Chuck," she greeted him, repeating his name for Liu's benefit. "Is everything all right?"

"No," he declared tersely, somehow making it less than one

syllable. "We need to go into the Magh Meall tonight before any more rakshasas can come over."

Martinez's fuzzy brain sharpened, picking up the nuance in his tone and choice of pronoun. "What makes you think more are coming over?" She could hear road noise in the background, meaning Yi was already on the move.

"I found out that the wards are still intact and they are escaping the Outer Lands with the help of a demon. If there is a gateway or portal in the middle lands, you'll need my help to shut it down," he informed them with a directness that bordered on rude. Luckily, Martinez had a thick skin.

"Do you know which one?"

"No, but all demons are bad. There are no gray areas here," he reasoned.

"How did you find all this out?" she quizzed him.

"From an old friend. The information is good. I'd stake my life on it," he vouched.

Martinez's gut was swayed for now. "Assuming all that is true, we still have a problem. We can't enter the middle lands until 13'o clock, which is"—she consulted the wall clock—"sixteen and a half hours from now."

"I can get us to the middle lands tonight," he assured her without giving details.

Woah. Martinez ran through the order of operations in her head. "Okay, but I still have to coordinate with the Ojibwa shaman to find a guide to show us where the rakshasas traveled."

"I'm headed your way. You've got two hours to reach out to them," Yi stated simply.

Martinez glossed over how he knew where they were and asked the question that intrigued her more. "What happens in two hours?"

"I'm going into the middle lands, with or without you two," he insisted. He heard Martinez audibly sigh over the sound of his tires riding the rough road.

"We're in Baraga. Let me make a few calls and get back to you on where to meet," she negotiated. He grunted acceptance to her terms and hung up—he hated using the phone while driving.

"What was that about?" Liu curiously asked.

"We need coffee, stat. And plenty of water and food for later. We may be going into the Magh Meall tonight," Martinez gave her the high points. As lead on the mission, it was her call, and if a demon really was backing the rakshasas, things just got a whole lot hairier.

Liu grabbed her wallet and the room card to get supplies while Martinez phoned in the situation. She dialed the direct line for immediate contact to Leader's proxy, usually but not always LaSalle. It wasn't saved on anyone's mobile or written down on a scrap of paper anywhere for security reasons, but every agent had it memorized for times like this. The line picked up on the second ring, and LaSalle's crisp tenor answered, "This is LaSalle."

"It's Lancer. I'm making an audible. We have third party intel that a demon is assisting the rakshasas' travel. The Korean shaman known to us as Chuck is going into the Magh Meall of the Upper Peninsula tonight. We intend to accompany him."

Chapter Sixteen

The Outer Lands
Summer Epoch

Faye slinked through the fragrant woods, her pack sleeping far behind her. She remembered the way to the cave mouth, although the journey seemed farther in the dark without the company of her sisters. Thrice, she had considered turning back and finding comfort in their collective warmth—was life under Popo's leadership really so bad? Then she remembered the bitter taste of the pack's dead and pressed on.

Walking the same path under very different circumstances made Faye pensive. They had been so hopeful and excited when they embarked, especially Lin. As an initiate, she hadn't been allowed to eat in the first few hunts, relegated to watch and learn how to be one with the pack from her elders. Faye remembered the sheer delight on Lin's face when she bit into her first human. Then the image of her lifeless body with a hole in her chest flickered involuntarily in Faye's mind's eye.

To stave off morose thoughts, she rehearsed her speech as she wound through the tall trunks. She knew she had to choose her words carefully; their benefactor was ancient, and like Popo, had survived by hiding in the shadows and playing it safe. The rakshasi didn't want to overstate how much a pack under her leadership could yield, but she needed to entice the demon into giving her a chance.

If Faye could convince the Old One to grant her access to the tunnels, her new pack could dine on well-groomed, lean meat instead of musky gristle. They too had the eyes the demon wanted, and they certainly tasted better. Faye wasn't sure what the demon did with the eyes, but she considered pitching urban eyes as higher quality.

Faye had never seen the demon—Popo had always conducted the negotiations herself with a few of her most trusted confidants—but she knew she lived in the steaming caves. It was a place shunned and avoided by most inhabitants of the Outer Lands because the Old One had garnered an infamous reputation. The demon was the bad guy in the stories monsters told their children. None of the pack had dared enter the caves until Popo's alliance.

Faye found herself on the edge of the tree line, staring at the entrance of the grotto. To one side was a small pool fed by an underground hot spring, giving the caves their name. There was a constant but erratic drip as the water condensed on the ceiling and fell back into the pool. The warmth of the enclosure beckoned her to enter, and Faye stepped into the humid cave. She was not going to throw away her chance this close to the Old One's chamber.

The moonlight only penetrated the first few feet of the cave, with just a shimmer of light reflected off the edge of the water. Rakshasas had exceptional vision in low-light conditions, but even to Faye's eyes, she could see no more than five feet in the preternaturally dark cave. Behind the pool, there was passage that led deeper into the black. Faye had briefly flirted with the idea of entering the mortal realm directly. Could she remember the way? Would it even be possible without the Old One's permission? Even her daring had its limits.

Faye stood outside the passage and looked at the orbs she held in her hand. Lin's eyes stared back at her. She'd palmed them during the mourning feast, and it hadn't been difficult to keep them hidden from the others. There was plenty of meat, with as many as had fallen. Faye mentally asked Lin's forgiveness as she placed the eyes on the ground just inside the entrance and in so doing, tapped the trip lines that ran across it.

The Old One was not an entity to be beckoned lightly, and the wait seemed an eternity to Faye's raw nerves. Then, the rakshasi heard clicking. Her ears perked up but the acoustics made it difficult to pinpoint how far away it was. Faye sniffed the air and knew she was not alone.

What business do you have with me, little one? Faye heard in crystal clear diction. It didn't reverberate against the walls like all the other sounds in the cave, and Faye shivered at the implication—the words hadn't been spoken aloud.

Faye wasn't sure if the demon could read her thoughts, but she didn't want to invite such practice and spoke loudly. "O venerable one, I bring you a gift and a proposition." She saw a red chitinous limb sweep Lin's eyeballs deeper into the cave and held her breath as the demon assessed her offering. The rakshasi could hear gnashing and grinding but couldn't see what was happening and didn't dare step any closer for a better look.

I accept your gift, the same voice rang in her head. *What is your proposal?*

Faye continued verbal communication. "You have given passage to some rakshasas to enter the mortal realm. I would like to lead such a group," she declared.

The demon kept to the shadows and probed the bold rakshasi standing in front of her. *How many in your pack?* she asked.

Faye spun the relative weakness of her position, "I would like to build a troop tailored to hunt humans in the cities, where the quantity and quality of meat and eyes is higher." Faye couldn't be sure, but she thought she heard the Old One laugh at her response.

You knew what to bring me. You must have already crossed into the mortal realm. What of your pack? the voice in her head questioned.

"We were ambushed and sent back to the Outer Lands," Faye answered truthfully. "I do not see much of a future with them."

In the mortal realm for over a moon and they only sent back eight eyes, the demon chastised. *Only to be turned back by humans. How embarrassing*, she condescended.

A chink appeared in Faye's confidence. "How did you know that?" she demanded.

I see many things, the Old One replied. *Like a lone rakshasi that has strayed from her pack. One that used her sister's eyes as a bargaining chip and won't be missed by her leader.*

Faye's hairs stood on end and she sprinted for the outdoors. The Old One hurled a net at the rakshasi in mid-flight. Her aim was true, ensnaring Faye's limbs and tail, throwing off her coordination. It was the split second the demon needed to pounce on the rakshasi from the shadows. The Old One sank her fangs into Faye's back, and the warm venom coursed through her with each rapid beat of her heart.

Faye's body went involuntarily limp, but she could still feel things: a hard landing as the demon dropped her to the ground, vertigo as she was rolled and trussed into a bundle, and every bump of the cave floor as she was dragged through the tunnels. She could still smell things: the acrid scent of the Old One and the stale odor of dead things. When Faye stopped moving, she heard the demon cut through the covering over her face and saw a serrated red tip.

It was the last thing Faye saw. With surgical precision, the demon popped out the rakshasi's eyes and cleaved them from their sockets. Paralyzed, she couldn't scream, but she howled in her head; the demon heard it nonetheless as she savored each juicy orb. The spheres exploded with the slightest pressure, like over-ripe grapes.

"Ssshhhh," she chittered out loud. The susurration was both eerie and comforting. *It will be over soon*, the demon promised.

Chapter Seventeen

Baraga, Michigan, USA
21st of November, 10:30 p.m. (GMT-5)

Rosaline Stillwater appraised the motley crew standing on her stoop as she peered through the curtains. Tracy Martin had returned with two Asians in tow: an old man in robes and a younger female with short hair. If it were anyone else, she would have sicced Pickles on the lot of them, but the maybe-marten had the boon of the forest bestowed on her by a noozhe-makwa manidoo. It would have been irresponsible not to help. When she opened the door, the Yorkshire Terrier didn't bark but growled low in his register. His menace was a warning: you have to get through me first.

Pickles recognized Martinez from before, but the others were unknown and smelled different. As a small creature, his initial instinct was to be leery of new things until he'd given them a good sniff. Stillwater did nothing to stop him from doing his job, and when he eventually backed down and returned to his warm doggie bed and smoked pig ear, she allowed them to enter.

"Thank you for agreeing to meet with us at this hour on such short notice, Ms. Stillwater," Martinez acknowledged the inconvenience of her request.

"Balance must be restored and everyone must do as they should," she replied neutrally and led them to the circular dining room table. "I didn't have much time to prepare, but there are more to power the ceremony."

"The collective will is greater than the sum of its parts," Yi spoke stoically.

Stillwater nodded in agreement but did not break her concentration. "Have you brought the asema?" she asked Martinez, who produced a baggie and placed it in the medicine woman's hands. Stillwater rolled out her sacred bundle and handed Martinez the rattle drum once more. "Just like before. Keep the beat steady. Don't talk until I tell you," she quickly briefed Martinez before addressing the others at the table. "And even then, only her," Stillwater gruffly insisted. The maybe-marten had already shown humility and eloquence with the spirits, but she wasn't so certain about the other two. They had strong wills, but the medicine woman didn't know the caliber of their strength.

Stillwater closed the bedroom door so Pickles wouldn't interfere and returned with a ceremonial shawl draped around her neck and a fat roll of bound and dried sage in her hand. She placed an ashtray in front of her and set the desiccated leaves alight. Martinez rolled the rattle drum between her hands while Liu and Yi sat quietly and focused their will on Stillwater's voice.

Her invocation was in Ojibwe, but they could feel her will

unwind and interlaced their own with hers, forming a lattice that bridged to the spirit world under her guidance. At key pauses and breaks, Stillwater sprinkled some asema on the smoldering smudge, adding a woodiness to the sweet smoke.

The drone of the rattle drum and the medicine woman's entreaties were like an earworm crawling its way into the noozhe-makwa manidoo's ear. The great she-bear fixed her attention to the source, and the tantalizing aroma drew her in. In the blink of an eye, she was inside Stillwater's dining room.

"Who calls me from the great forest?" she growled—had she not just answered such a summons? The medicine woman gave Martinez a nod.

"Forgive me, great noozhe-makwa manidoo," Martinez pulled out what little Ojibwe she knew to properly address the supernatural creature. "I have come to inform you that the invaders have been sent home and balance has been temporarily restored. However, there is a festering wound that needs to be healed. I seek a guide to show where the invaders came from so the way may be sealed."

The wispy form carried such gravitas that the smoke seemed weighty. "You do not come alone, maybe-marten." The manidoo considered Liu; there was no doubt she was a fierce hunter, but the bear found no wickedness in her heart. Then the manidoo turned to Yi and was momentarily awestruck by what she saw. The light of his being shined bright through the distance between worlds; it was almost painful to look at, like staring directly into the sun. "And what are you?" she pondered as she nudged him with an ephemeral paw.

"One who wishes to ensure balance is maintained," he answered truthfully. Stillwater gave him a sharp look, and he quieted.

Martinez spoke up, "He is familiar with the invaders' homeland and can sever the unnatural connection that brought them here in the first place."

"You have such skill and knowledge?" the noozhe-makwa questioned Yi.

"It has been a long time, but this is not the first I've heard of such creatures," he replied after tacitly clearing it with Stillwater. "If possible, we would like to go tonight, before they have time to regroup and send more over."

The great she-bear considered the proposition. She was a stalwart protector over the great forest, and the idea of allowing more outsiders into her domain irritated her deeply, like an itch in the center of her back that she couldn't quite rub against a tree. However, the maybe-marten had been true to her word. When her mind had been made, the noozhe-makwa clapped her paws together. Everyone at the table viscerally felt a ripple of power course through them as the manidoo manifested something from the spirit world into the mortal realm. The piece of shaped bone clattered on the table. It was six inches long and an inch wide, and the edges were curved like the wings of propeller. A piece of braided sinew was attached to one end and wrapped around its slim width.

"Let it breathe the life of the middle lands. Kitchi-Sabe

will hear its sigh and come to show you the path you seek. Do not linger longer than you must; the woods are especially dangerous at night." With that note of caution, the manidoo left them, and there was a lightness to the smoke once more.

Martinez resumed the rattle drum while Stillwater closed the way between worlds, formally thanking and praising the generosity of the noozhe-makwa and the goodness of Kitchi-Sabe, just in case he was listening in. Stillwater stubbed out the smudge stick in the ashtray and took off the prayer shawl. Martinez placed the rattle drum on the table and put on a pair of gloves before picking up the bullroarer.

Intellectually, she knew it was simple aerodynamics, a mere weighted airfoil that made a hypnotic drone that could change pitch by altering either the rotation speed or the length of the attached cord. However, her inner child longed to unravel and spin it round, as one does with noisemakers. The low-frequency sound could travel long distances and while it was associated with Australia's indigenous tradition, all people around the globe had some form of the wind instrument. She ran her fingers over the smooth surface decorated simply with notches.

"That was wild," Liu marveled and motioned with her hands. "She was right here—no wards or circle. She could have ripped my head off if she wanted to."

"There are many ways to practice the arts," Yi replied, unfazed by the experience.

Stillwater pointed to the Liu and stated with authority, "*She* is a marten—feisty, curious, a little arrogant, and a natural hunter." Liu took it as a compliment and bowed slightly. The medicine woman then addressed Martinez, "But I know now, you are no marten. You are something different."

Stillwater put her finger to her lips and reassessed Martinez in light of the company she kept. She chose her next words carefully and extended an invitation. "If you want to know your true name and color, come back when you are done. When you know who you are, you know where you belong, where you are going, and where you came from."

Martinez diplomatically smiled. "Thank you for that honor, but I know enough to do what I must and I do not need to know more." Stillwater and Yi were both taken aback by her response and surety, and Liu fought the urge to give her a fist bump under the table.

"As for you," Stillwater turned her attention to Yi. "You had one job—keep quiet and focus your will."

"Isn't that two things?" Yi asked rhetorically with a hint of mischief.

"Keep talking, and I won't let you use my fire pit," she threatened. They stared off to see who would break their impassive mien first, and Martinez cleared her throat when the stalemate persisted longer than was socially comfortable.

"A thousand apologies. I meant no offense," Yi eventually surrendered. "I have been left to my own company for too long and have forgotten my manners."

Stillwater harrumphed as she rose. "You're lucky I like her," she motioned to Martinez and let Pickles out to do his business before her visitors laid claim to the backyard. Rather than waste more time driving into the wilderness, Martinez had asked to use Stillwater's backyard. They needed someplace safe that could be purified with fire and water, and she had a private space with neighbors that were used to her practice. The medicine woman had agreed; she had no interest in walking the middle lands herself, but she was curious to see how it was accomplished.

Yi started unpacking his ritual tools while Liu and Martinez tried to keep a straight face at the geriatric, shamanistic version of flirting. Martinez added the bullroarer to the rest of her gear: night vision goggles, her Glock loaded with banishment bullets for Asia, a spare magazine covering North America, and the compass. She'd cleaned the back with salt and baking soda before loading it with a few hairs from the rakshasi's tail—the rest of it was packed in salt in their hotel room, awaiting transportation back to the Mine.

She patted down her pockets and found her magic-boosting rosary where it should be. She had her saltcaster just in case, but it was all but useless in the Magh Meall. Everything there was magical, and there was too much static to glean any one specific signature. Her hand grabbed the charms hanging from her neck. She kissed the crucifix and Saint Michael pendant that her mother had given to her and verified by touch that the amber periapt that protected her from being targeted by magic was still around her neck. Once she'd finished her gear check, she started hydrating and loading up on sandwiches in anticipation of a long trek before she could eat again.

Liu, who had checked her knives and filled her bandolier at the casino, was already a sandwich up on Martinez without signs of slowing. For someone so small, Liu could pack away a surprising amount of food. She handed Martinez a ham and cheese while she filled up the grounded canteen to the brim.

Entering the Magh Meall at night was a first for both Salt Mine agents. They had always entered the proscribed way: find a secluded spot, trench a circle, light candles on the four cardinal directions, crumble a ring of shortbread, and spend an hour of meditation before entering when the clock struck thirteen. They had always arrived at the height of the afternoon, and neither had had occasion to stay until it was dark. When they had presented their supplies to Yi, he laughed and ate the shortbread himself, reassuring them it would not be needed.

Once Pickles was back inside, Yi stacked the fire pit and kindled the flame. He cleansed the area with fire and water before making a wide circle—Martinez, Liu, and himself inside and Stillwater outside. He whipped his white fan open and fanned the air inward while he cast his will. Martinez and Liu reinforced and wove their will around his, making a dome around them. Yi cued Liu, who struck the gong exactly thirteen times while Martinez shook the cluster of bells. She wondered if she was getting a reputation as the percussion section in shamanistic rituals, and if that made her the Ringo of the group.

Stillwater watched the display with intense interest and in

the blink of an eye, they were gone and the night was quiet. She diligently kept watch on the circle, waiting for their return.

Chapter Eighteen

Magh Meall
Summer Epoch

Martinez's stomach floated up into her chest before bottoming out again. It was like the worst airplane turbulence times ten. She managed to keep her sandwich down—although barely— and when her equilibrium returned, the cool night air of the mortal-realm Upper Peninsula had taken a turn. It was now warm and green and smelled like chasing fireflies through a field barefoot. She opened her eyes and saw the great forest of the UP in its supreme form.

Everything was more vivid in the Magh Meall, and it was easy for mortals to become distracted or intoxicated in the buffer zone between the home of fae and man. The dirt never smelled so clean nor felt so real as it did in the middle lands, and every tree was the absolute paragon of tree-ness. The moonlight spilled through the cracks in the canopy, and its hue was almost golden yellow. The collective respiration of all the plants created a gentle breeze as they waited for the sun to rise and cast a lavender tint to the light and the land.

"Is everyone okay?" Yi checked in with Martinez and Liu.

They both nodded in the affirmative. "Now I understand why we usually spend an hour crossing over," Liu added as she pulled out one end of a ball of string from her pocket and tied it to a metal stake. She drove it into the ground with a firm stomp. Ariadne's string was enchanted—as thin and strong as silk and undetectable to any passersby. It was Liu's personal anchor back to the safety of the circle, which was particularly useful when she was chasing something in the Magh Meall. She generally had a good grasp on pathing, but the geography of the middle lands didn't always follow the rules. She didn't know how long the string was, only that it had never run out on her, and she had personally tested it out to two miles.

"You ready to call the guide?" she asked Martinez, who had her night goggles on and her glock on her hip.

"Let's do this," Martinez said resolutely and unraveled the bullroarer. She gave the cord a few feet before gently rotating it around. As she spun it faster, a vibrato filled the night as the piece of bone whipped through the air. She varied the speed and let a little more cord out to lower the frequency for a wider broadcast, and it wasn't long until they saw a form emerge from behind a tall, wide oak.

The notion of Bigfoot was nothing new to Martinez. There was enduring affection for sasquatch in the Pacific Northwest, and its distinct silhouette graced many a bumper sticker, t-shirt, and logo, but nothing could prepare her for seeing one in the flesh. He was human shaped but covered in fur, and least eleven feet tall.

Liu instinctually reached for a weapon, but Martinez made a fist and gave the hand signal for her to cease. His steps were quiet due to his padded wide feet, and Martinez had no doubt that he could pass by them unheard if he wished. She interpreted his choice to make noise as a welcome. Liu keep her hands free but close to her bandolier.

Martinez let the bone piece slow in its rotation and shortened the string to keep it from hitting the ground before addressing him. "Thank you for coming, Kitchi-Sabe. The noozhe-makwa sent us to heal the wounds left here by the wanton hunters. Could you show us the way they took?"

The giant took a knee and held out his oversized hand. Martinez placed the bullroarer within as proof of her claim. His large, round, deep set eyes examined the token, giving Martinez time to take a better look at his face. It was definitely hominid but not human. The sabe closed his hand and nodded. He rose to his full height, turned around, and starting walking.

Martinez picked up her pack and motioned for the others to follow. She took point while Liu guarded the rear, and Yi found himself sandwiched between them. Aware of the shortcomings of his companions, the sabe shortened his stride and slowed his gait, occasionally snapping a fallen branch so they could follow his lead.

Despite his great size, the sabe loped through the forest with ease; it was his home. To the Ojibwa, he was the embodiment of one of the seven sacred grandfather teachings: honesty. The sabe was thought to be closer to the Creator than humans, and when he walked among people, it was a reminder to remain true to the natural forms bestowed to them by the Creator. Only by accepting and being true to one's spirit can one be honest, and veracity—in speaking and action—was essential to living a moral existence.

Martinez stayed focused on their guide and cast her will wide as she went, heeding the she-bear's warning. As a magician, she could practice the arts in the Magh Meall, and since it was a place made by the fae, there was no karmic debt when it came to wielding magic. Additionally, a little magic went a long way, and if she did need to throw down some serious will with her rosary, the effects would be amplified. That wasn't to say magic was free and clear. The Magh Meall took its toll in other ways, as many a mortal that wandered into its realm unaware and uninformed discovered.

Although it was created by the fae, other supernatural beings lived there as well. The fae were a whimsical folk that enjoyed the drama that came with mixing things up among all sorts, and the only exception to this penchant was fiends. Demons and devils were prohibited from entering the Land of Fae, and they took an active dislike to any that may have been wandering the Magh Meall.

This truism made Martinez think that this unknown Asian demon wasn't necessarily a fiend and perhaps instead a poor cultural mistranslation for an entirely different supernatural creature. It wasn't always clear-cut who was a faerie versus a mere resident of the middle lands, especially for someone that didn't subtextually understand the creature and the culture that named it. Of course, that was an irrelevant academic point tonight. Whatever it was, it certainly didn't belong here and if they came across it, a banishment bullet or a slice of Liu's banishment blades would send it back to its native realm.

Kitchi Sabe led them out of the tree line and into a clearing. It must have been a significant or holy place on the mortal realm, because that was the only time the forest of the middle lands broke. A large shadow swept by out of the corner of Liu's peripheral vision, and she called an alarm, crouched low, and grabbed a throwing dagger. Yi and Martinez took cover in the tall grass, but the sabe stood his ground.

As the shadow came back over them, they saw the wide wings of a bald eagle glide across the clearing. The white of its head and tail feathers gleamed in the moonlight, and its hooked yellow beak and sharp talons were none too comforting. A ferocious screech blared out as it came for another pass. The sabe cupped his mammoth hands around his mouth and called back. The eagle swooped down low for a better look; it came so close that Martinez could see its piercing eyes sizing them up. Due diligence done, the eagle caught an updraft and soared onward, leaving them on their way.

Kitchi Sabe motioned for them to rise, and he continued

his trek through the field. They had walked for an hour when he stopped and pointed at a cluster of boulders. There were no nearby mountains or cliffs that could have accounted for rocks of such size, but this was the Magh Meall; it didn't have to make geologic sense. The mute giant resolutely sat on his haunches and wouldn't approach any closer.

Martinez pulled out the compass, and the needle stayed fixed on the rocks, regardless of her position. "I think this is it."

Liu picked up a small rock and chucked it into at the cluster. The projectile hit true and clattered against the stone. "It's not an illusion," she surmised without the risk of wearing sunglasses at night.

Yi admired her ingenuity and stepped forward. "Let me take a look," he offered. The shaman summoned his will and saw that which his eyes could not see: a doorway that both existed and didn't exist. He pressed his vision beyond the rocky surface and saw a cave entrance roughly six feet in height, tall enough for a rakshasa to comfortably pass through. As his supernatural senses ventured further, he realized that what he saw was no longer in the Magh Meall. The air was cold and loomed with jeopardy.

"We are at the right place," Yi confirmed and grabbed a piece of rope and his ceremonial dagger. "I have to sever the metaphysical connection before I can backfill the entrance."

Martinez and Liu looked at each other to see if that made sense to the other. They came up blank, but now was not the time for explanations. "What do you need us to do?" Liu asked.

"Stand guard and be ready to attack anything that tries to come out," he said as he donned his black robes—wisdom to hear what was being said and understand how he was supposed to act upon that knowledge. "It took a lot of time and will to make this portal, and if its creator is inside, it won't be happy that I'm trying to close it."

Martinez pulled out her gun while Liu had a throwing dagger in one hand and a runed serrated hunting knife in the other. The sabe had their rear with no signs of running away.

Yi steadied his mind; what he was about to perform was no gut. There would be no gong strikes, bells, or melodious song to draw the demon's attention. There would be no purification of fire to draw its gaze, but Yi did sprinkle a little water from the grounded canteen to purify himself with water.

He held the rope out and grafted his will into its fibers on one end, creating a metaphysical extension of pure magic. Like a cook making noodles by hand, Yi stretched and pulled out his will until the ropey strands were long and pliable. The shaman braided them into a strong cable and hurled the fabricated rope into the portal. The short segment in Yi's hand went taut as it passed through the rock face, and suddenly, the cave entrance was visible to everyone. Despite the sudden change, Martinez and Liu remained on alert—that was magic; expect the unexpected.

With the rope now bridging two realms, Yi unsheathed the

dagger and spoke words of power as he sliced through it. After he sympathetically severed the connection, the release of arcane energy blew back at them, momentarily flattening the blades of grass. An unearthly scream echoed from the cave. Martinez and Liu kept their feet and focus while Yi moved onto the second part of his plan: summoning an earth elemental.

Elementals were old beings, largely considered passe among modern practitioners but they were not without their utility. As the living embodiment of a specific element, their abilities were largely environmentally dependent. For example, fire elementals could control flames and wind elementals could fill sails in otherwise still seas. Like constructs, they obeyed simple commands, but results varied the more complex the directions. It was a matter of being very specific and asking the elemental to do exactly what was in its wheelhouse and no more.

The shaman quickly threw on his red robes to invite the spirit world to interact with him. He grabbed his collection bells and shook them at a brisk and frenetic beat. He started singing loudly, calling the earth itself to rise up.

The wind picked up, swirling across the tips of the tall grass. The rocks rolled toward each other and stacked themselves into a vaguely humanoid form: a torso with two arms and two legs and a head. The gale tightened into a vortex, picking up dirt in its wake. It piped the soil into the cracks, mortaring the individual rocks together into a cohesive unit. Then, it plastered mud onto the head, giving it facial features. Martinez had never seen an earth elemental before, and she wasn't sure if the two red pinpricks were actually giving it sight or simply there to let its summoner know it was online and facing him.

There was skittering and movement in the shades of black within the cave, and Liu tore her eyes away from the stony hulk. "Whatever you're going to do, do it fast."

Yi stilled the bells, and though his short stature did not change, his shadow grew as he gave the elemental its command: fill the cave with earth until you reach bedrock. A blink of recognition flashed in the red light of its eyes, and the motile amalgam of rock and dirt leapt into the opening. Almost instantaneously, the cave entrance disappeared from sight, and the rock face was uniform once more. The levitating rope went slack and fell to the ground. The gusts died down to a steady breeze, and there was no more sound coming from the rock formation.

Martinez motioned to Liu to keep cover while she checked the compass; the needle spun freely without focus. "I think it worked," she said for the benefit of her companions.

Liu put her blades back and patted the shaman on the back. "Chuck, you don't mess around."

Yi gave her a tired grin and sat on his heels. "You got some water for an old man?"

Martinez pulled the grounded canteen from her pack and joined them in the grass. The stars sparkled like diamonds in the sky, heightened by the adrenaline that was coursing through their veins. Martinez wondered if the constellations were different in the Magh Meall and found herself wishing she knew more about astronomy.

Behind them, the sabe rose and cautiously approached the cluster of boulders. He stayed an arm's length back and extended a long, thick finger. He poked the rock a few times and found it solid. A broad grin spread across his face and he chortled. As long as Martinez lived, she would never forget the sound of a sasquatch's laughter.

Chapter Nineteen

Detroit, Michigan, USA
22nd of November, 12:15 a.m. (GMT-5)

The mood in the sixth-floor library of the Salt Mine was decidedly exasperated. On the whole, being the Salt Mine's librarians was a pretty good gig. Chloe and Dot had access to an extensive esoteric library in a safe setting, and their work had purpose outside of the pure pursuit of knowledge. They had trained many agents in their time, each uniquely gifted in their ability to understand and practice the arts. And when no one required their help, they had the run of the place to themselves. It was like being on a permanent sabbatical even if they were always on-call for esoteric questions and emergencies. Some days, it was easy work. An agent sent in their head scratcher and one or both of them instantly recognized it—done and dusted. And then there were days like this.

The twins had been going full steam after Martinez had reported running into their favorite Korean Yooper shaman and he'd identified the perpetrators as rakshasas earlier this afternoon. Like Yi, Chloe and Dot thought the entire lot was in exile, and their return to the mortal realm was unexpected and disturbing.

They knew the basics on a wide number of esoteric disciplines, but when it came to Asia, the twins were definitively at a disadvantage. Many of the primary sources were either lost or on the other side of the planet, and neither librarian liked to rely solely on translations and secondary or tertiary sources. Magic was about subtextual understanding, and language was a window into how a culture thought and expressed itself.

Even when they'd learned the language and studied the culture, it was challenging to adjust for the inherent bias toward those with a written script. For example, there was more to East Asia than the Chinese, but its script was so old, its written records the most numerous, and its influence so extensive that learning Chinese gave them the most bang for their buck. And then there was the way things were recorded; historical records were largely told through the victor's lens with heavy doses of propaganda against the vanquished. That problem wasn't exclusive to Asia, of course, but its relative distance from the western culture they were most familiar with made it that much more difficult to tell fact from fiction when it came to the supernatural. Historians had a difficult time telling which was which when it came to mundane matters: Chloe and Dot's job was significantly harder.

The fact that Martinez and Liu had banished the rakshasas and sealed the passage with Yi's help bought them some time, but there were still too many unanswered questions. The new signature found in the cabin wasn't in the system, and the possibility of demonic involvement was concerning. All fiends were a pain, but if the twins had to pick one, they'd take devils over demons any day. Demons were chaotic evil incarnate; at least devils kept their word and the problem lay in litigious loopholes and things subject to interpretation. They had Asian contacts they could reach out to if they felt they'd hit a real brick wall, but until that point, they'd keep searching for the needle in a haystack.

The librarians had decided to divide and conquer, with Chloe hitting the Sanskrit-based texts while Dot focused on the Chinese ones. Unfortunately, their search hadn't yet yielded results and when they started bickering more than usual from a bad case of the hangries, Chloe had the bright idea of getting takeout in theme with their research. Dot knew her sister well enough to know she was only picking Chinese over Indian because of the fortune cookies. She had lost count of the number of times Chloe had hailed it the perfect meal because "it comes with its own sweet end." Personally, Dot thought that was a lame cop-out for not having a proper dessert like gulab jamun.

Dot picked through the remains of the double pan-fried noodle with her chopsticks, hunting down any rogue pieces of beef or noodle swimming in the soupy dregs at the bottom of the oyster pail.

"I think there's some Buddha's delight left," Chloe

commented as she ate the last steamed dumpling and stacked another empty box to the side away from the books.

"Or, I could do this," Dot answered contrarily. She picked up the container of white rice and started scooping the sticky clumps into the flavorful, greasy juice.

Chloe smirked and poured another a cup of tea for Dot to cut the oil. The surly blonde silently accepted the gesture against future indigestion, not that it stopped her from shoveling the saturated rice into her mouth with chopsticks. With their hunger sated, the conjoined twins resumed their respective reading side by side as they had lived their entire lives: Chloe on the right, Dot on the left.

Having eidetic memories was extremely useful in navigating the world of runes and sigils and learning different languages, especially logosyllabic ones where one couldn't just learn the alphabet and sound out words. Essentially, Chloe and Dot could recall an image from memory after seeing it only once without enhanced cognition techniques. It was often erroneously conflated with having a photographic memory—which ironically had no visual component—and Dot was quick to correct that error in even the most casual conversation.

The brusque blonde would also point out that science hadn't found someone with a true photographic memory, whereas eidetic memory was real, if rare. Eidetikers were almost exclusively children, and they usually lost the ability as their language skills developed and they relied less on visual stimulus.

For the twins, however, it remained well into adulthood. Sadly, having exceptional memories didn't give them all the answers, but it did make finding them easier.

Retrieving memories was largely an unconscious process, the most simple being recognition—the brain letting you know you have previously experienced that thing before, akin to a cranial reflex. Actually recalling something was the coordinated neural reconstruction of a memory—complete with context— from different parts of the brain. It was the difference between passing someone on the street and knowing you knew that person versus knowing their name and *how* you knew them. When one had read as many books and seen as many things as Chloe and Dot had, there were a lot of faces to recall, so to speak.

They leveraged their skills by employing various methods anyone could employ to enhance their memory and recall. First, they ensured good encoding of information, which meant studying materials with minimal distraction and in some logical framework so the new knowledge would have interconnectivity with similar topics. While raw recognition did not provide context, it could be enough to activate an entire network of memory.

Second, they strengthened their memory by specializing according to their personal interests. Not only did this allow them to cover more ground, but it made their memory more durable. It was a truism every teacher understood: students retained more information if they made more connections and found meaning in a subject, rather than reading something because it was assigned.

For example, they were both fluent in Latin, but Chloe preferred Liturgical and Dot Classical. When they had to perform a ritual to Janus earlier this year, Dot was lead on the litany, but when a question concerning Medieval Latin writings came up, Dot deferred to Chloe. In so doing, they strengthened the neural pathways for their own niche within Latin because the more a memory was used, the more important the brain thinks it was. The end effect was they were able to move information between long-term memory and working memory more effectively when it came to their areas of expertise.

Chloe closed her current book and grabbed another fortune cookie. As there were accounts of rakshasas in Hinduism, Buddhism, and in Jainism, there was a lot of ground to cover. As a whole, rakshasas were pretty insular, and if they worked with others, it was either because they had shunned their maneating ways or the arrangement allowed them to slaughter and eat more. She snapped the crisp cookie in half and glanced at the slip of white paper tucked inside. It was a teach-yourself-Chinese one, showing the character for beer and how to pronounce it, but it still had lotto numbers on the other side. She crunched on the vanilla wafer and, fortified with a little sugar, picked up another spine.

Dot cracked her knuckles and moved onto her next book:

Chuan Mizang or *Transmission of the Mystic Store*. It was written in the tenth century BCE by the Buddhist scholar-official Zanning and detailed esoteric Buddhist practices during the Song Dynasty. Dot was particularly interested in the incantations, or *dharani*. These spells were heavily influence by Vedic Sanskrit and were typically spoken in Buddhism, but the Chinese had a penchant for writing them down or inscribing them on objects to use as protective charms.

There were two kinds of dharani: nengchi and negnzhe. The first were incantations designed to hold onto good dharmas, lest they be scattered or lost. The types of things were categorically similar across all cultures through time, even if the particulars changed—good health, prosperity, fecundity, etc. Dot was more interested in the latter, which aimed to block evil or bad desires. In her experience, what a culture feared was generally more telling about their unique worldview. Sure, some of those demons were manifestations of intangible unrest, but sometimes, they were real monsters.

Dot flipped through the volume detailing various recitations with instructions on how, when, and to what end each should be employed. Every so often, she would grab the printout of the picture Martinez had sent over to compare the runes, but nothing seemed to fit.

The hollow circle Martinez had found in the cabin was crude and bare bones, and frankly, perplexing. The width of the circle was a function of how many runes you had to include to perform the magic safely and the physical size of the thing inside the circle. When it came to supernatural creatures, size was not always indicative of their power or how much havoc they could bring down in the mortal realm. If the rakshasas were summoning a being into the mortal realm, they didn't feel the need to protect themselves from it or bind it to the circle, and at six inches in diameter, it couldn't be another rakshasa.

The other option was that it was a sending circle. Instead of summoning something into the mortal realm, the rakshasas were sending something out. Any security measures would be on the recipient's end, which would allow for fewer runes and a much smaller circle. Like any piece of mail, it had to have some sort of name or address, either of which would narrow the search considerably if the twins could catch a break.

Dot turned the page and scanned the next spread; something pinged in her head. She darted her eyes back and forth from the circle to the book—it was close but something was off.

"Did you find something?" Chloe asked hopefully as she bookmarked her place—she could note the smallest change in her sister's demeanor. Dot wasn't the sort to get giddy, but she was almost smiling. Chloe found the gleam in her sister's blue eyes promising.

"Maybe," Dot answered cautiously. She pulled out a thick permanent marker and started tracing the lines on the print out. Chloe waited patiently and let her sister do her thing. "If this is a sending circle, what if these symbols weren't drawn to be read by the sender, but the recipient?" Dot proposed as she flipped the paper over, and placed it beside her book. The black permanent marker bled through to the other side, and she grinned wide. "We have a name: Yanjing Jugui," Dot intoned.

"Which means?" Chloe asked.

"A ghost or demon that takes eyes," Dot did her best to translate the ideas behind the characters. "According to Zanning, this incantation will protect your sons during 'the inauspicious season.' When it is written in the blood of a sacrificed animal on one's skin or on paper that is braided into a bracelet to be worn on the right hand, it hides the protected individual from the demon's sight."

Chloe sat up and looked at the circle with new eyes. She felt a tickle of a memory and sifted her thoughts. "There is a story about Vishnu in his Rigvedic avatar Varaha; that's the one where he's a boar," she spoke as she grabbed a different book from the pile on her side of the large circular desk. "He lifted the Earth out of the cosmic ocean and of course, it was infested with all sorts of evil things, so he went on patrol," Chloe went off her memory until she found the right passage.

Chloe changed her cadence and translated the passage. "One day, he saw a demon with many eyes threatening the goddess earth. Its two-lobed black body skittered on ruby legs with frightening speed, and venom dripped from its terrifying fangs. Varaha saw evil in its multitude of eyes and charged the monster. His tusks struck true but they failed to penetrate the hard protective shell of its body. The demon turned its attention to the boar, but Varaha did not flee from its hideous countenance. He charged again, this time aiming for its ocular cluster. The monster howled in pain as his tusks gouged out one of its eyeballs."

Chloe skimmed the rest of the passage, which, like many epic stories, was repetitive, self-referential and used poetic language. "So basically, Varaha attacks the demon a bunch of times until it's blind. It tries to escape by burrowing into the ground, and Varaha starts digging after it but can't rout it out. He chases it into the bowels of the earth until he had passed into another realm." With that she set the book down and pointed at a sigil written into the margins. "Look familiar?"

Dot held up the traced circle and found it a match. "So we have a Chinese Buddhist creature with a Sanskrit Hindu address," she sighed. "What happened to the demon?"

"No idea. The story focused on Varaha, who backfilled the hole once he resurfaced. He then knocked up the goddess earth, and had to be killed by an incarnation of Shiva when he and his three boar sons started tearing everything up on earth," Chloe summarized. "But, I may have a picture," she perked up with her usual optimism and pulled out a different book.

"Angkor Wat is covered with bas reliefs depicting the battle between the devas and asuras for control of the Earth," she explained as she placed the open book between them. There were two figures, the four-armed man with the long snout and tusks that was Varaha, and a giant spider that must have been the demon. "The ancient Sanskrit roughly translates to 'eye reaper' or 'one who harvests eyes,'" Chloe added.

"That rolls off the tongue better than eye-taker demon," Dot muttered. "So rakshasas are sending eyes to the harvester of eyes, possibly in exchange for passage into the mortal realm? How did they even meet if it was ousted from the mortal realm before rakshasas were even a thing?"

"The Outer Lands?" Chloe speculated. "The harvester of eyes dug itself to safety; who knows where it got to since it was blinded by Varaha?"

"Apparently, it took a pit stop to tenth century China," Dot retorted. "But if it had the means to travel to the mortal realm, why not just come and hunt itself? Or kill the rakshasas and take their eyes?"

"Safety?" Chloe guessed at the first question. "Rakshasas typically belong to clans or hunt in packs, but if the harvester uses them to hunt humans and they send it eyes, it comes out ahead with very little personal risk."

"Maybe they have to be male human eyes?" Dot hypothesized about the second. "Or Song Dynasty Chinese didn't give a squat if their daughters lost their eyes."

Chloe shrugged. "Do demons ever make sense?" she asked rhetorically.

"No, but it means this thing could be bigger than thirteen

rakshasas and five dead people in the Upper Peninsula," Dot surmised. Chloe picked up the phone to call for reinforcements while Dot started searching her memory for more references to Asian monsters interested in eyes.

Chapter Twenty

Melaka City, Malaysia
22nd of November, 2:55 p.m. (GMT+8)

The corporate office of the Bertuah Mining Company was stuck in the Friday afternoon doldrums. The experienced employees knew how to stretch their work to give the appearance of productivity right up to the end of the day, in contrast to the eager youths that had no sense of pacing. They would sprint to finish tasks just to twiddle their thumbs in boredom while they waited out the clock.

Everyone knew better than to openly chatter about their weekend plans and instead took the conversation to social media and messaging, sneaking progressively more frequent glances toward their mobiles. The telltale signs were all there: downturned heads, tapping thumbs, and a volley of pings. The office manager said nothing as they were on target and they had the decency to try to conceal their activities. Civility must be rewarded.

Like most mining in Malaysia, the Bertuah Mining Company was foreign-owned. It had started over a hundred years ago as a British endeavor and rose to prominence with the demand for tin, particularly during the World Wars. Even after Malaysian independence in the '50s, it remained in British control, protected by the universal sanctity of commerce. When the decline in both price and ease of extraction of tin occurred in the '80s, the company diversified into other products, and the metallic mineral subsector currently produced tin, gold, bauxite, iron-ore, as well as the saleable byproducts of tin and gold mining.

No one knew what to expect when the British owners sold the company last year to a multinational corporation, but most counted on another old white guy in a suit taking over—or maybe his son. Instead, they got Kanali Patel as their new regional director. She was Indian, more specifically Tamil, and late middle-aged with just a bit of gray in her long wavy black hair that was always tidily pinned up or back. At first blush, she looked like one of the ubiquitous aunties that all Asians grew up with, complete with the penchant for sweets and plenty of sugar in her chai. At five-foot-five and 160 pounds, she was hardly physically imposing, but anyone who dared challenge or cross her soon discovered a depth to her icy stare and commanding tone.

As with any transition of power, there was an adjustment period. Patel pruned the unproductive staff but kept the rest. When she did hire, she pulled from local talent instead of bringing in her own people from abroad. She showed no preferential predilection for hiring Indians over any of the other many ethnic groups that formed the mélange of Malaysia. The office consensus was that Patel was firm and disciplined, but fair. She ran a tight ship, and as long as things were done on time and to her specifications, she had few complaints.

Patel adjusted the small fan on her desk to circulate the stale, moist air in her office. It was perpetually hot and humid, and the start of the rainy season last month only exacerbated conditions. She dipped a rock-hard Parle-G biscuit into her tea and expertly pulled it out just before it had a chance to break and fall back into her cup. Sweet tooth satisfied, she turned her attention to the projected budget for next year.

There was always a mountain of paperwork and reports to review, either from one of the various mine operations or from the construction of their new corporate headquarters in an old tapped-out old iron mine in the foothills just outside the city. The idea to convert a dead mine into usable space was one of the first initiatives Patel spearheaded as regional director, and miraculously, everyone was on board. Brand management was excited about putting a new eco-friendly face to the company via the inclusion of a mining museum on the premises. The staff was looking forward a new facility with more office space and ample parking, and the accountants were counting the zeros that would come from the sale of the current offices, thanks to the steep appreciation of land prices in the city center.

Melaka City was a thriving coastal river city with a rich

history as a trading port over the centuries. With a population of half a million, it was both the capital city of the state of Melaka and the oldest Malaysian city on the Straits of Malacca. Melaka City embodied the Asian fusion that was indicative of Malaysia while also bearing traces of Portuguese and Dutch occupation in their food, customs, and architecture, to say nothing of the British influence. All of Malaysia had been a British colony at one time.

In the late '80s, Melaka City was declared a historical city, home to both the oldest Hindu temple in Malaysia, the Sri Poyyatha Vinayagar Moorthi Temple built in 1781, and the oldest traditional Chinese temple, the Cheng Hoon Teng Temple erected in 1673. As soon as the city was designated as a UNESCO World Heritage Site in 2008, lots of money went into restoration and tourism became big business, which drove up real estate prices, especially in the historic areas. It made sense to move the corporate offices to cheaper land that wasn't otherwise producing income, but that didn't make logistics any less difficult.

The first few bars of a ringtone broke the restless quiet of the office, and everyone looked around to see who the offender was—personal calls during work were frowned upon. Much to their surprise, it was coming from the regional director's office. The more curious employees wondered who was calling their boss in a personal capacity; she was known to be an unmarried, childless career woman. Seasoned staff kept their heads down and didn't ask questions.

Patel put down her customary afternoon tea and answered her mobile. "This is Kanali Patel," she answered in English.

The voice on the other line was male, precise, and to the point. "We need an assist." Patel recognized the voice immediately, although its typically crisp diction was a little slack and tired. She consulted her watch with a flip of her wrist and did the time zone math; it was the middle of the night in Detroit. "Are you ready for me to patch you in to Leader for briefing?" LaSalle inquired.

"Just one moment," she replied as she rose from her desk and shut the door to her office. A susurration of speculation arose from the other side, but she paid it no mind. She had more important concerns than wagging tongues, and the wards were activated once the door closed. When she was back in her seat, she gave LaSalle the go-ahead.

There was an audible click, a few seconds of hold music, and then another click. Patel reflexively straightened up in her seat as she had done for numerous briefings in Leader's austere fourth-floor office. Distance did nothing to diminish her authoritative voice, "Prism, we had rakshasas in the Upper Peninsula that entered the mortal realm with the help of an Asian demon that collects or takes eyes. The rakshasas have since been banished and the arcane passage closed, but I'm sending Lancer and Aurora your way to follow up on the demon. I need you to do some ground work in anticipation of their arrival in

Kuala Lumpur."

"Of course," Patel replied. "Have LaSalle send me what information you have and I will make the appropriate inquiries."

"Chloe and Dot have come up with a name in Chinese and a location in Sanskrit," Leader filled her in.

"Then it's a good thing Little India and Chinatown are right down the road from each other," Patel said neutrally.

"Lancer is lead on the operation, but she isn't one to dismiss council or assistance," Leader obliquely laid out the chain of command.

"Understood," Patel reassured her long-term employer. "Just send me their ETA, and I'll take it from here." She reflexively bobbed her head side-to-side and made a twisting gesture with her hand which Leader perceived in spite of it being unseen.

"I expected nothing less from you," Leader replied. Patel had worked long enough for her to know that was a resounding compliment.

With the exception of Deacon, Kanali Patel—codename Prism—was the oldest and longest serving Salt Mine agent. During her twenty-seven years of service, she had banished, summoned, captured, retrieved, or neutralized more supernatural things than she cared to remember. She had trained many agents over the years and had outlived many of them—*Hail Vishnu*. Unlike Deacon, who would prefer to die with his boots on, the reality of field life had started to lose its charm for Prism. Despite her growing ennui, she'd pressed on with her work; being a Salt Mine agent wasn't exactly a job from which you walked away.

Leader could see the mileage stack up on Patel, and she hated to lose such an asset to boredom or attrition, which is why she'd offered her the chance to relocate to Malaysia for a long-term assignment with more executive tasks instead of fieldwork. Patel jumped at the opportunity, not the least to avoid another Michigan winter. She had always been a creature of the sun, and a dip below 70° F was considered a cold day this close to the equator.

When the Bertuah Mining Company became a subsidiary wholly owned by Discretion Minerals through a series of shell corporations, Kanali Patel arrived in Melaka City as Regional Director. The corporate transition wasn't difficult thanks to her business background and the capable administrators and advisors she kept on to ensure that she had time to concentrate on her real assignment: establishing the Iron Mine.

The Iron Mine was a new branch of the Salt Mine, charged with assisting in the acquisition of Asian esoteric knowledge and widening the surveillance network for magical malfeasance in the region. Patel still had access to the Salt Mine's analysts, the librarians, and Weber, but as a regional office, she was also building something from the ground up on her own. It was both exciting and daunting.

Although there were mining operations all over Asia that

could have been used as a front for arcane operations, Leader specifically chose one in Malaysia. Malaysia welcomed foreign investments, had a stable non-totalitarian government—officially a federal constitutional elective monarchy—and it had untapped potential in the natural resources sector that had largely been ignored in post-colonial times. As a former British colony, it had a high rate of English literacy and their legal system had its roots in English Common Law, even if caning and flogging were still on the books as punishments. Malaysia understood how to do business with the west, but remained solidly Asian in temperament, which was crucial to the embryonic Iron Mine.

Malaysia was truly pan-Asian in scope, and gave the Salt Mine access to many cultures from one geographic location. It had maritime borders with Thailand, Singapore, Vietnam, Indonesia, and the Philippines, and a long history of trade and settlement with the Chinese and Indians. The majority of Malaysians practiced Islam, the religion of the Federation, but the constitution established Malaysia as a secular state that granted freedom of religion. In essence, they were all Malaysian, but individual groups were allowed to hold fast to their ethnic and religious roots. Unlike the homogenous vision of the American melting pot, Malaysia was very much a stew. No one had batted an eye when Patel joined Malaysian Indian groups or questioned the Institute of Tradition's mission to preserve cultural heritage.

Patel didn't have to wait long for the encoded message that popped on her phone with a name—Yanjing Jugui or netra zasyacchid, depending on which Asian community you asked. The location of said demon was less than helpful: in Sanskrit, it translated to "accursed lair of the harvester of eyes." Patel sent off a quick message before gathering her possessions and informing her office manager he was in charge for the rest of the afternoon. Next year's budget could wait; she had a demon to hunt down.

Chapter Twenty-One

Melaka City, Malaysia
22nd of November, 6:45 p.m. (GMT+8)

Muhammad Mukarto Che downshifted his Audi and slammed on his brakes as traffic slowed ahead of him. Driving headlong into the city center on a Friday night wasn't exactly his idea, but duty called. He'd been overseeing the construction of Bertuah Mining Company's new corporate offices, as well as the covert esoteric section, when he got Patel's message—it'd sent a chill down his spine. He'd always assumed the tale of demons that stole your eyes was something parents told their kids to scare them into behaving.

The longer he spent working with Patel, the more the line between fact and fiction blurred. Others would have fled from the truth, but he was never one to turn a blind eye to unpleasant things. How could he be happy in ignorance? Perhaps that was why Patel had hired him—she needed someone who wouldn't run away from the light, even when it revealed horrific things.

Che could only think of one person in Melaka City who would know more about such things: Seri Dini, the half-human daughter of the naga Seri Gumum. She was said to be astonishingly beautiful but willful; both traits that strained her relationship with her mother, who prided herself on her own allure and the rightness of her thinking. To be fair, she was a majestic dragon, and Che wondered how much bravado it must have taken a man to mount such a magnificent creature.

Eventually, Seri Dini left her mother's waters to find her own, and she currently resided in Melaka City's Chinatown. She found the great abundance of waterways soothing to her serpentine divine half, while her humanity dined on the spectacular food and drama that mortals created without thought.

Nagas were magical beings with a strong affinity for snakes, said to have the ability to take the full or partial form of a serpent. They originated in an enchanted subterranean realm filled with earthly treasures, but when humans came into existence, their curiosity got the better of them. Those that left their native realm traveled through water, and when the waters receded, they became stranded inland, much like Seri Gumum, who swam Chini Lake in Pahang.

Nagas had a bad reputation in monotheistic western religions where everything divine that wasn't God was labeled a demon. Their domains were called "Hell," and their motivations were broadly assumed to evil. What else could one expect from religions that chose the serpent to typify the temptation that brought on original sin? However, they were held in higher esteem in the polytheistic faiths of the east. Nagas were often seen as a protagonist in Hinduism, and there was more than one four-armed god that was depicted as wearing a serpent around the neck or waist.

Although Seri Dini wasn't evil, she was old and powerful, and Che had advised Patel to wait for him before venturing into Chinatown. He'd given her a list of items to acquire while he wrapped up at the construction site, buying him time before she lost patience and went in solo. She probably would have been fine, but he'd grown inexplicably protective of his employer over the past several months. At five-foot-six and 150 pounds, he wasn't a big man, but there was a definitive grit about him; his opponents might win the fight, but he was going to hurt them badly before he went down.

Che cursed the congestion and took a sharp turn right into the backstreets. It was a longer, more circuitous route but would ultimately take less time. The Audi slowed down as it neared Little India, which was nothing more than one section of a street with a few Indian shops and restaurants. It was modest compared to the ones found in larger Malaysian cities like Kuala Lumpur or Penang, but it was enough to make sure Indians in Melaka City could get the food, music, media, clothes, and brands that reminded them of home. He spotted Patel at a fry shop eating pakoras.

Patel was a strict vegetarian, and she knew better than to go hungry into Chinatown where pretty much everything would have meat except the desserts. She recognized Che's car on its first pass and watched it turn to circle the block; the roads were a maze of one-way streets. She began the process of politely extricating herself from the intricate details of the owner's daughter's recent betrothal. By the time he made his fourth circuit, Patel was waiting for him. He pulled his car to the curb and turned on his hazards.

"Mukarto," she greeted him upon entry.

"Ms. Patel," he replied.

She settled into the leather seat and buckled in. "Let's go to Chinatown."

The first thing Patel had done when she got into town was find an assistant; ideally, a local magician who understood the boundaries and balance of Malaysian society that could plug her into its esoteric network. She'd scoured the city's many religious structures and cultural centers, but ultimately found her assistant playing a heated game of mahjong in the back room of a high-end club that catered to clientele with more money than sense. Unlike those in his immediate surroundings, he wasn't loud, obnoxiously drunk, or hyper aggressive, and there was a resolve to his quiet demeanor. Still waters ran deep, and there was a something churning under the tranquil surface.

Che was Malay in the strictest sense of the word. His family descended from the Austronesian peoples inhabiting the Malay Peninsula long before the Chinese, Indians, or Europeans found their shores. He spoke many languages, including Malay, and professed the religion of Islam, which made him a Bumiputra

Malaysian for anyone who put stock in such designations. His family was wealthy, but not rich, and as the youngest of five sons, he drew the short stick when it came to divvying up resources as to who was sent abroad for school and work.

However, he hardly had a life of deprivation. He was educated at the best Malaysian schools and universities, and as the fifth in line, he was given a wide latitude. Despite his mother's best efforts, he remained unattached and had become an accomplished practitioner under the tutelage of a bachelor uncle. Being a magician was a dicey proposition when it came to his more religious family, but he was the first person they called when they needed help.

Che steered away from town to cross the river at any junction that didn't involve the roundabout in the heart of historic city center. It would be packed with tourists headed toward the Jonker Street Night Market and locals that should have known better. "How are things at the site?" Patel asked once he was out of the worst of traffic. Until construction was complete, the Iron Mine was housed in Patel's place, with a warded, salt-lined chamber to store any recovered magical items awaiting transportation back to the Salt Mine.

"Everything is on schedule," he reassured her as he pressed on the clutch and up-shifted. "Did you acquire the offerings?"

Patel answered by patting her bag. She'd followed Che's instructions to the letter, down to the specific brands: a particularly smoky Lapsang souchong tea, a fragrant sandalwood incense, and a bag of ginger flavored Ding Ding Tong, a rock hard candy that literally had to be chiseled into bite-sized chunks. They skated the edges before entering the older, seedier part of Chinatown on the western bank of the river. There were progressively more Chinese characters on the signs, pagodas filled the skyline, and in the distance, they could see the streamers and lights of the Night Market.

In a feat that defied the laws of physics, Che parallel parked in an impossibly small space, and the pair walked to the noodle house. The raucous din of crashing mahjong tiles, cups slamming on tables, and Cantonese spoken loud enough to travel across rice fields spilled out of its open doors. Che entered before Patel, and the noise promptly died down as they sized up the newcomers. The noodle house was an institution in Chinatown, but it wasn't a place listed in any travel book. It was for locals of the Chinese persuasion.

"Better to eat rice than flies," Che said in Cantonese, subtly suggesting they should close their proverbial gaping mouths and mind their own business. All the Chinese Malaysians spoke Mandarin—it was the language of the Chinese government, education, and business—but at home and amongst friends, people often spoke in dialects: Hokkien in Penang and to the north, Cantonese in Kuala Lumpur and the south.

Patel readied her will in case things took a turn for the worse, but the hiss of water hitting a hot wok broke the stalemate. This was the noodle house, and if the kitchen was still cooking, it was business as usual. The bustle resumed, and Che ushered Patel through the labyrinth of tables and chairs. There was a persistent haze of aerosolized oil that penetrated every particle. The smell of frying minced garlic bloomed in the air as they approached a beaded curtain.

The sounds of the noodle house's patrons diminished as they walked down a long corridor, past the toilets and supply room. At the end was a closed door, muffling the sounds of a cinematic score playing on the other side. Che reached to knock but stopped when Patel stayed him with a heavy hand on his shoulder. She swept the entrance with her will and saw the unseen protections in place. "We should be safe as long as we have no intent to harm our host," she replied and removed her hand. Che nodded to show his comprehension: no weapons but keep your magical defenses up nonetheless.

He rapped three times, a firm and decisive knock on the solid door. The music cut out and a female voice called out, "Who's there?"

Patel amplified her words through the door with her will. "One seeking the insight of the daughter of Seri Gumum." She felt a force probe her from within, and she stood firm, giving it neither entrance nor assault. It seemed like an eternity to Che while the women magically squared off. He could feel the raw energy in his proximity, like a downed electric wire that was still live. "We bring gifts," Patel added after a minute.

The deadbolt clicked in its retreat. "You may enter."

The room was thick with smoke, a mixture of tobacco and incense. The scenic landscape on the large television that hung on the wall was frozen on pause. An ornate, pearl-inlaid screen divided the room so that those on either side could have a clear view of the TV. At the end of the screen was a table with a half-eaten meal, surprisingly not noodles.

A young Chinese woman no more than twenty was seated closest to the door. She was dressed in jeans and a sweater with her hair pulled back in an elaborate ponytail that was shaped like a bow. She tucked her phone away and pulled out a tray. "For your offerings," she said in flawless English; her voice lacked the necessary weight and will, which could only mean that Seri Dini was on the other side of the screen.

Patel laid out the tea, incense, and candy, and the young attendant carried it to the table. A hand floated out from behind the divider to examine them one by one; whoever had sent them knew what she liked, although she had since opened her palate to coconut Ding Ding candy, thanks to her young attendant.

Seri Dini flicked her tongue and tasted the air; there was power without malice. It had been a long time since anyone had evoked her linage, and she curious what brought them to her door. She addressed her helper officiously. "Go to the market and bring me back a Chinese burger with spam and a coconut ball."

"Of course," the young woman leapt at the request. This was

hardly how she wanted to spend her Friday night, and getting an hour reprieve was better than nothing. "I'll be back shortly," she fibbed. As long as the food was hot and the coconut fresh upon her return, did it really matter how much time she spent with her friends? Her thumbs were furiously tapping before the door had shut completely behind her.

"It will be at least an hour; her boyfriend works at the stall next to the coconut stand. Youth these days…" Seri Dini chided. "Now, what have you come to ask me about?"

"Yanjing Jugui," Patel spoke without mangling the tones.

"Who better to ask about a demon than another demon?" she mused from behind the screen with a rattle of her tail.

"We know that nagas have no inherent predilection for evil and are guardians of their waters," Che spoke in Malay. The phonemes rolled into her ears, and she was transported to a time long since passed.

"And what has she done this time?" the naga hissed.

"She created a doorway for rakshasas to re-enter the mortal realm in exchange for eyes," Patel spoke simply.

The daughter of Seri Gumum chuffed, and her laugh had a distinctly serpent quality. It was rather disquieting. "That's a new one," she responded.

"Anything you could tell us about her would be a great help," Patel added.

Seri Dini lit a cigarette and adjusted her long body on the chaise lounge. "You two better take a seat. It's a long story."

Che pulled a chair out for Patel before taking a seat. They sat facing the screen.

"She wasn't always like this. Before humans came, she was a protector of the land, but she didn't take it well when a new world order came. Suddenly there were a bunch of creatures calling themselves gods and claiming dominion over land that was already inhabited. And bam, there were humans everywhere. It was a lot to take in…no offense intended," Seri Dini said as an aside once she remembered her current company.

"None taken," Patel graciously replied. "Sometimes I can hardly stand them myself." A lilting giggle came from the other side of the screen.

"Anyway, she'd had enough when this new divinity came around and started calling herself Goddess Earth." She switched perspective and languages and rattled off in Cantonese, "I have eaten more salt than you have eaten rice, she told the new goddess, albeit in different terms." Che grinned; he had a soft spot for Cantonese idioms.

"Getting blinded and driven below ground added injury to insult, and she grew sour in her isolation. The wounds never healed properly and she festered in her bitterness, staying clear of the mortal realm and hunting exclusively in the Outer Lands, for eons. That all changed when she came across a human who walked the in-between lands. His flesh was subpar and immature, but his eyes granted her vision of a sort. It was limited, but she was no longer blind. That's when she started digging tunnels." Seri Dini paused to take drink and a long drag.

"Tunnels to where?" Patel asked.

"Everywhere," her host answered. "She avoided the Indian subcontinent because that was where she was blinded, but she hunted all over Southeast Asia: China, Cambodia, Laos, Vietnam, Myanmar, Thailand, Malaysia." Patel was amused at the naga's notion of "everywhere"; she *had* spent a long time with the Chinese. "She stalked humanity, not for food but for sight. It got so bad that the gods had to intervene, limiting the frequency of her trips into the mortal realm. Every forty-nine years, she was allowed one moon to take forty-nine eyes."

"So why use rakshasas if she could hunt herself?" Che spoke. "Ninety-eight missing eyes every century in a population composed of a billion people is a drop in the bucket."

Seri Dini shrugged, a gesture her guests could not see but the subsequent rattle of her tail bore the same ambivalence. "I'm not sure. I think her last foray was roughly thirty years ago in Myanmar. Or maybe it was the time before that…was it still Burma then?" she searched her memory and couldn't pin it down. "As you can see, we don't keep in touch, and she knows better than to hunt around my waters."

The gears in Patel's mind were turning and a Machiavellian plot was unfolding. The harvester of eyes had a network of tunnels connecting different Magh Mealls that no one else dared to use because she was a pissed-off primordial giant spider. She was limited in how often and how many eyes she could take, but if she had someone else supply her eyes—no harm, no foul. Rakshasas traveled into the mortal realm under their own supernatural power, but had been effectively banned in all of Asia for ages. If the harvester of eyes could get them to a non-Asian Magh Meall, the rakshasas could feast and she could have a steady supply of all the eyes she wanted. It was a win-win, except for humanity.

"We know Varaha blinded her, but who imposed the restrictions upon her the second time?" Patel inquired.

This, Seri Dini had no problem recalling. "Lord Vinayagar defeated her. Some say he took pity on her and allowed her some leeway. Others think it was demonstration of dominance over something that was impossible to kill. She *is* older than time."

"Which do you believe?" Patel asked. She could feel the semi-divine being on the other side of the screen ponder her query.

"Why not both?" she petulantly answered. "Always one or the other with your kind."

Chapter Twenty-Two

London, United Kingdom
23rd of November, 8:05 a.m. (GMT)

Martinez and Liu were both looking down at their phones when their food arrived: two full breakfasts. They had a three-hour layover at Heathrow before their flight to Kuala Lumpur, and they'd parked themselves and their special issue luggage in a secluded corner of the restaurant with plugs to charge their mobiles.

Liu looked up first, and her stomach growled at the display of fried, baked, grilled, and toasted food placed in front of her. She started on the black pudding and caught Martinez's furrowed brow in her periphery.

"More good news?" she asked sarcastically. They had traveled many miles over the past day: a nine-hour drive back to Detroit, a quick pit stop at their respective homes and the Salt Mine for a change in supplies, and an overnight flight to London. They were monitoring the influx of information, and Prism's latest intel on the Harvester of Eyes was less than reassuring.

"Aaron wants to know if I'm allergic to cats," Martinez

puzzled aloud.

Liu's left brow raised. "Why?"

"Not sure. That's what worries me." Martinez tapped out a quick reply and put her phone away. She considered the mounds of meat that had arrived. "Maybe this was a bad idea,"

"You'll thank me when we get to Kanali's," Liu cautioned. "She has no problem with people eating meat on their own time, but there won't even be eggs in her pantry." Martinez nodded and tucked in, adding slices of grilled tomato and mushrooms to her sausage and eggs.

Martinez had turned the situation around, and it was a bear of a task no matter how she looked at it. Now that they had a better idea of what was going on and which magical signatures to match to, they could better surveil for rakshasa activity. The only problem was that it was a de facto reactionary position, like a giant game of whack-a-mole. They would always be chasing the cause after the effect, and that didn't sit well with her. There was no doubt in her mind that focusing on the Harvester of Eyes was the way to go, but the question was how, and the fact that Chloe and Dot didn't have answers put her on edge.

The Salt Mine was generally not bothered by the existence of demons as long as they didn't mess with the mortal realm. The standard operating procedure was containment and banishment, and Martinez had packed more Asian banishment bullets accordingly. However, if the Harvester of Eyes had extensive tunnels leading to different Magh Mealls, banishment didn't really accomplish anything. It wasn't the same as banishing the rakshasas back to the Outer Lands where they couldn't re-enter the mortal realm on their own.

It was theoretically possible to kill demons, and Liu had brought her special blades just in case that became a viable option, although their power wasn't as clear-cut as banishment blades. The tougher the fiend, the harder it was to erase them out of existence. If the half-naga was right, the Harvester of Eyes wasn't some simple imp they could snuff out without a second thought. Liu was good at what she does, but Martinez didn't think she could do what a god with no less than four arms couldn't. The non-descript gray and glass of Heathrow did little to lift her mood. The bacon helped.

Her phone pinged, and she breathed a sigh of relief. "It's Wilson. He wants to bring his cat to Thanksgiving, if that's okay with me."

"Wilson got a cat?" Liu exclaimed in disbelief. "I didn't even peg him as a plant guy, much less something that required feeding *and* a litter box."

"It's better than what I feared. I thought Aaron was going to buy me a cat for company once he moved out," Martinez tapped a quick *kk*.

"Your Thanksgiving dinner is filling up. Now we have to kill this demon and wrap things up on time. Chloe and Dot will be so vexed if they miss out on deep-fried turkey, and you know Aaron will burn the backyard and house down if you're not there," Liu joked as she picked up a piece of toast from the rack and buttered it.

Martinez wearily chuckled. "I know monster hunting is your jam, but I don't know how you can be so nonchalant about this."

Liu pointed her butter knife at Martinez. "It's all in how you look at things." She dipped the end into a pot of Marmite and spread a thin layer on her edible canvas. "While we are stuffing our faces with five different kinds of protein, the twins are working five hours behind us and Prism eight hours ahead. Something is going to shake out. And we got new bling." she alluded to the protective charms the twins had given then before they left Detroit.

"If you think about it, we've got it easy for the next sixteen hours," Liu said philosophically, swirling the savory black spread to the corners. "There is literally jack squat we can do until we meet up with Prism, so we might as well eat up and get some sleep on the plane." She bit into her toast with a satisfying crunch.

"Okay, I can buy that," Martinez conceded—there was little point in wringing her hands. "But aren't you a little daunted about going up against something older than time?"

Liu sipped her coffee. "We'll go with the best play we've got. That's how it always is, regardless the opponent. We don't have the option to sit by and let things fall apart. When it's go time, just channel your inner Hobgoblin and go balls to the wall. If your ticket is punched, at least you'll go out trying to do some actual good in the world. How many people can say that?" she asked rhetorically.

"I think you're in a meat-fueled fugue state," Martinez jabbed her arm. "You just evoked Hobgoblin in some very Zen sentiments."

"Credit's where it's due. Dude's a yahoo is so many ways, but he lives in the moment—chop wood, carry water," Liu responded. "But you are not allowed to tell him I said nice things about him. That's the last thing his ego needs."

Martinez smirked. "Your secret is safe with me."

Chapter Twenty-Three

The bell over the temple rang for evening prayer. Everyone was welcome, believers and tourists alike. There were plenty of signs to guide the uninitiated. Take your shoes off and wash your feet before entering. Refrain from loud conversation or horseplay. Please, no touching the shrines and statutes.

It had been a while since Kanali Patel had been to the Sri Poyatha Moorthi Temple. She was a devotee of Vishnu, and the temple was dedicated to Lord Vinayagar, the one-tusked elephant-headed god with the rotund belly also known at Ganesha. He was the remover of obstacles, the patron of the arts and sciences, and the deva of intellect and wisdom. With an axe and noose held in his upper arms, he was also a slayer of demons.

Unlike denominations or sects in monotheistic religions, Hindus were generally cool with other Hindus worshipping a different god or goddess than them, but Ganesha even more so. As the god of beginnings, all Hindus invoked Ganesha at the beginning of prayers, religious ceremonies, and important undertakings. He is often portrayed as dancing, and in south India, performances of the arts often began with an invocation to him.

Freshly bathed and dressed in modest clean clothes, Patel slipped off her shoes and washed her feet, symbolically leaving her ego behind before she entered the sacred space. While others made the circuit and started at the side altar to the left, Patel headed straight for the back of the temple where the priests had dressed and prepared the shrine for worship and kept the sacred fire burning.

Patel joined her palms at the level of her heart and bowed deeply at the waist and then at the knees. She presented her offering: a box of small fried balls of dough sweetened with honey and topped with slivered almonds. It was customary to bring Ganesha *modaka* or *laddus*, although a more generic gift, like fruit or flowers, would also have been graciously received. In the iconography, his trunk swerved to his lower left hand to investigate a bowl of sweets.

The priest accepted the laddus on Ganesha's behalf and recited a mantra over her—*Om Shri Ganeshāya Namah*. He then poured holy water over her hands from a small brass pot. Patel reflexively touched her bindi, her nose, and her mouth. The priest moved on to the next supplicant; it was his job to care for the shrine and pray to Ganesha on their behalf, not unlike an intercessor.

Patel repeated the mantra and threaded her will into the

syllables. It wasn't so much a summoning as a metaphysical poke to get Ganesha's attention within the safe confines of the holy space. To see and be seen by the divine was the heart of Hindu worship. For those that had little exposure to the supernatural, any little thing could be construed as being seen by the gods, and they could go home with a sense of well-being. However, Patel knew the difference between a rogue wind and the gaze of the divine.

The devotees came and went, but Patel stayed and called out to Lord Vinayagar, he who vanquished netra zasyacchid. She was unaware of how much time had passed, so deep was her meditation. Finally, she felt a tap on her shoulder.

"What troubles you so that you spend hours in evening prayer?" a voice curiously asked. It was male, mid tone, and rather lyrical. Patel did not have to open her eyes to know it was not a mundane priest that spoke. She wasn't even sure if this conversation was really happening. It was entirely possible that it was taking place in her subconscious.

"I seek the wisdom of Lord Vinayagar concerning netra zasyacchid," Patel answered without looking up.

She felt his chuckle in her gut; round, deep, endless. "Worry not, daughter. She is bound and her terror has limits."

"If only that were the case," Patel softened the correction. "She has found a way around her confinement and uses rakshasas to do her bidding." Her reveal was met with silent skepticism.

"And what would you have Lord Vinayagar do about such a thing?" he questioned her playfully. "The age of devas battling demons is long past."

"Perhaps, but there are mortals who have taken up the mantle," Patel said diplomatically. "We are at the beginning of a thing. Who else would I pray to?" she said coyly. She felt his gaze zoom in on her.

"You wish for him to remove obstacles?" he guessed.

"Or place them where they are needed. Some beings must be kept in check," Patel answered. "I would not deign to ask Lord Vinayagar to do anything that was not in accordance to his dharma."

The humbleness of such a bold request intrigued him. He was accustomed to people asking for elimination of all impediments, regardless of the trivialness of the endeavor. "You speak with a wisdom beyond your years," he complimented her.

"I would gladly receive any knowledge Lord Vinayagar would bestow upon me. Netra zasyacchid is an old and fearsome quarry," Patel fished for information.

"Ask yourself, why does such a lifeforce need human eyes?" he posed the question. "Was she not able to hunt and eat in her blinded state?"

"She wanted to expand her vision—to dig tunnels to new places? To see what was going on in the mortal realm?" Patel ventured.

She felt a hand on her head and his breath in her ear. "Know that you have been seen. There are limits to what even the gods should do, but go with my blessing." He pressed a cloth sack into her hands. "Take this *prasad*, and when you are ready to face your foe, use it to draw Kraunsha to you. He has a knack of getting into the most secret places undetected. When you have blinded netra zasyacchid once more, call my name and I will put appropriate obstacles in place."

Patel felt lightheaded when the weight of him left her, and she was glad she was already on her knees in prayer. She opened her eyes to the dressed statue of Lord Vinayagar. It looked the same as before, but she was certain it watched her now. She checked her hands and found the prasad still in place.

The priest who had taken her offering earlier came over to her. "My apologies, but evening prayer is over."

"Of course. Thank you for letting me stay so long," she replied as she rose.

"Some prayers need more time. You are welcome to return in the morning," he offered with a non-committal sideways bobble of the head. The temple was open every day for morning and evening prayers.

"*Nandri*," she answered in Tamil and took her leave. Her shoes were the last in the stack of cubbies, and halfway down the street, she realized she was quite ravenous. It was well past sundown, but the buildings and street were lit up for the night market. She checked her watch: 9:15 p.m. Instead of returning to her car, Patel detoured to a *chaat* stand she knew was not far away.

The nice thing about Indian street food was that they came in two basic categories: veg and non-veg. It took the guesswork out of eating. She never had to wonder if that stall used chicken stock in the vegetable soup or if fish somehow didn't count as meat. She ordered two *vada* and the aroma of the rice and lentil donut frying in the hot oil made her mouth water. It came with two cups: one filled with *sambar*, a vegetable stew cooked with *dal* and tamarind broth, and the other with coconut chutney.

Patel carved off a bite-size piece with two spoons, cutting through the crispy exterior and the fluffy insides. She dropped the chunk into the spicy soup and waited patiently for the bubbles to stop, signaling complete saturation of the vada. She fished the soggy morsel out and liberally spooned coconut chutney on the top before popping it in her mouth. It was smooth, crunchy, spicy, and creamy all at once. She made quick work of the rest and pondered her position.

Patel had an entry. Prasad was a small sweet customarily handed out by priests after a *puja* or prayer, however this was no normal prasad. Kraunsha was Ganesha's rodent companion or vahana, often depicted at the god's feet or acting as his mount—what better way to attract a rat *vahana* than with divine food? She also had a containment contingency: call Ganesha. Hopefully he would respond faster than he did at the temple.

She was still a little fuzzy on how to find all these human eyes the demon had been collecting for millennia or how to blind something that was already blind. And there was no exit strategy, per se, but it was a start. Tomorrow was a new day, and her visitors would be arriving early.

Chapter Twenty-Four

Melaka City, Malaysia
24th of November, 9:45 a.m. (GMT+8)

"Kanali, you call this a house?!" Liu exclaimed as she slid out of the Audi and took off her sunglasses to appreciate the view. "Have you got some forced labor tucked away in the back? Mukarto, blink twice if you are here against your will."

"It's good to see you, too, Joan." Patel greeted her with a big hug. Martinez, who had only met Prism a few times shortly after hire, hung back with Che, who had picked them up from the airport in Kuala Lumpur. Martinez grabbed her bags from the back and joined the duo on the porch.

"Teresa, welcome to Malaysia," Patel addressed her. "Come in and get comfortable. I've set up your rooms, and breakfast is ready whenever you are. Take your time freshening up. You must be tired from all this traveling."

"What's for breakfast?" Liu asked.

"*Paranthas* stuffed with cauliflower and potato with *achaar* and chutney," Patel answered. Liu gave Martinez an "I told you so" look.

"That sounds delicious," Martinez replied. "Maybe we

could go over things at breakfast…." She used deliberately vague language because she wasn't sure if Che was just a chauffeur.

"No need to mince words in front of Mukarto. He's my assistant in all things and has been thoroughly vetted," Patel informed them. Che nodded and passed the ladies on his way inside with Liu's luggage in hand.

"You have your own LaSalle?!" Liu whisper-shouted. "Wait, does that make you the brown Leader?"

Patel gave her an enigmatic smile. "We'll talk over breakfast. Chai?"

Martinez left them to catch up and retreated to her room. After a cursory sweep, she stashed her gear with care. Having a gun without registration was a serious crime in Malaysia, and getting caught pointing a gun at someone got years of jail time, even if you didn't hit your target. But there was no way Martinez was going without her Glock, so the plan was to not get caught. She took a quick shower, changed into new clothes, and went downstairs for breakfast.

The paranthas were laid out in a stack with the chutneys and pickles on the side. A carafe of hot chai was on the counter, and the smell alone was invigorating. Liu and Patel were already at the table and greeted the refreshed Martinez.

"I almost feel human again," Martinez blithely commented.

"Nothing a little tea and food won't fix," Patel reassured her with a full plate. Martinez examined the contents. She had eaten her fair share of curries and naan, and she could eat the hell out of pakoras and samosas, but this was her first go at Indian stuffed breads. It looked like a savory pancake, but it wasn't fluffy like an American pancake or thin like a crepe. It had layers, similar to lamination but not nearly as flakey or buttery. There were bits of smashed potatoes, and flattened cauliflower inside. It was flavorfully spiced without being spicy in terms of heat.

"So what did you find out after you were touched by a deity?" Liu asked as she picked up her second parantha. Patel always cooked enough to feed a small army.

"You make it sound so creepy," Patel chided. "It was a blessing, and I have the beginning of a plan, but we have a few gaps," she admitted.

"Lay it on us," Martinez said between bites, and Patel started her account while the two younger agents ate. Liu dived in with gusto; she was the kid that mixed together all the soda flavors at the fountain to see what it tasted like. Martinez was a little more systematic.

She methodically cut up little bites and spooned a little of each chutney on a square. She tried the mint chutney first: green and fresh with just a little heat. Then the tamarind: sweet and slightly sour. Then the coconut—*dear Lord why haven't I been eating coconut chutney this whole time?* Martinez doubled down on the chutneys. Patel was amused at the methodical precision she employed. If she was like this with breakfast, she could only imagine what she was like with work.

When Martinez scooped a large spoon of achaar, Patel knew what was coming next and pushed the cucumber *raita* in her direction without pausing her narrative. Martinez flapped her arms like a chicken as the heat spread in her mouth and down her throat, and Patel liberally spooned her the soothing yogurt dish. Martinez made a note to herself—*stick to the chutneys*.

As Patel wrapped up her conclusions and thoughts, Liu patted her food baby and Martinez polished off the last bite from her plate. After that breakfast, even the Harvester of Eyes didn't seem so hopeless. Patel gathered their plates and brought out some fresh fruit for a sweet finish.

"Kanali, that was wonderful. You're the Indian mother I never knew I needed," Martinez declared as she popped a sweet flowery piece of papaya in her mouth.

Patel made a gesture of gratitude; a cook never tires of people liking her food. "I'm just sorry I wasn't there to greet you at the airport. Mukarto is dependable but he isn't one for chitchat."

"That's what phones were created for," Liu commented as she picked the cantaloupe from the bowl. "So, where do we go from here?"

"Well…" Patel dragged out the one syllable, "there are three of us, four if we rope in Mukarto. I thought maybe you could contact the guides and we could get a look at this accursed lair. See what we are up against."

Liu gave her a dirty look. "I should have known breakfast

was a trap."

Patel smiled sweetly. "Think of it as a bribe you didn't know you were taking."

"Am I missing something? You're great at divination stuff." Martinez asked

"Being good at something and liking it are two very different things," Liu clarified. "Contacting the guides is an emotional roller coaster. You are basically trying to convince three women—sisters, mind you—to do what you want them to do. It's all the work of being a lesbian three times over without anything to look forward to at the end."

"The way to your heart really is through your stomach," Martinez teased her. "Once, she helped me out for a pot roast dinner," she said to Patel and sipped her perfectly steeped and sweetened chai.

"I don't know where she puts it all. She's so small," Patel said with affected amazement.

Liu gave them a side eye. "If you two are done, I'll need candles, a reflective surface, and some incense."

"It's already set up in my ritual room," Patel answered evenly. "Will we need Mukarto?"

Liu gave it some thought. "No. It's always nice to have more power, but the guides will like the symmetry of three women petitioning them." The silent man nodded; if he took any offense, he didn't show it.

Patel led them to the meditation room that acted as her

ritual space with her assistant bringing up the rear. It was airy and bright, a vast departure from the dingy, cold basement Martinez was used to. As a general rule, Malaysian homes didn't have basements; the very idea of putting a hole into the ground under your house that could collect water, mold, and mildew was laughable. Plus, anytime they saw a basement in a movie, it was haunted by ghosts, so it was best not to chance it.

The circular table was set up for scrying with a large mirror in the middle and candles set up around it. The circle and runes had already been meticulously chalked in. Patel struck a match, set the incense alit, and blew it out once a smolder could be sustained. She stuck the ends of the sticks into the sand and proceeded to light the candles. Martinez drew the blinds to cut down on the light reflecting off the mirror. This was the one time a basement would have come in handy. Liu double checked the circle and took out her focus—three Chinese coins knotted to each other with red ribbon through their square centers. Che stood outside the door, ensuring no one disturbed the woman in their esoteric work.

When the three of them found their seats, they held hands, and Liu spooled out her will. She recounted the greatness of the guides, naming each in her litany. Was there any sound sweeter to the ear than one's own name? Patel and Martinez aimed their will into hers, making a braided plait of pure thought and energy. Like an expert angler with prime bait, Liu reeled the guides in with flattery and praise.

When a gray fog came over the mirror, Liu knew she had their attention. She creatively rephrased her request in the best light possible and raised her volume. "To the guides that watch over us, I beseech you to show me the lair of Yanjing Jugui, the demon who collects eyes, so that we may put those souls to rest and stop any other others from falling victim to her." The mist swirled, but there was no clarity in the mirror.

"Your intent is noble, but it is beyond our vision," a disembodied voice spoke. "Our link is with the mortal realm. It must be a truly accursed place."

The three woman exchanged looks; how had they not considered that? But Liu was never one to accept defeat lightly. "The demon has recently procured the eyes of a man not long dead. Perhaps you could see through his eyes still," she suggested.

There was a pause as the guides debated this. It was within their capability but a highly irregular request. There were times they entered the body of a medium, but it was a messy affair and put them out of sorts for hours afterward. And then there were the ethical considerations; the guides prided themselves on being fair and neutral parties. After conferring, they eventually decided there was no harm in trying since the human was already dead,

"Give us the name," the voice instructed.

Liu shot a darting look to Martinez, who searched her memory. The stripper still had his eyes, so the most recent deaths would be the pair of hunters. Assuming both sets of eyes were taken by the rakshasas and not eaten by a lucky crow… "Arnold Manning," Martinez spoke, taking the even odds. The mirror cleared and darkened but there was nothing in the glass, only blackness.

"Open your eyes to us, Arnold Manning," the guides commanded. Suddenly, the void filled with pinpoints of light. It looked like stars in the night sky, but there was no moon and they could see the curve of the cave ceiling. Lattices of fine silk gleamed as they crisscrossed the cavern, and the former eyes of Mr. Manning saw no less than six exits—holes whose entrances were covered in webs.

"What are the points of light?" Martinez whispered. She doubted they were bioluminescent insects or fae given that the Harvester of Eyes was a giant spider with webs everywhere. They could have been mineral or crystal deposits in the rock, but where was the light they were reflecting? Of course, if could always been something as simple as magic but why would a blind spider need light?

"Is there a zoom or 360 on this thing?" Patel muttered under her breath.

Liu smiled but wiped it away before addressing the guides. "Could we see more of this place through Arnold Manning's eyes?"

The sisters repeated the request in the strangest game of telephone Liu had ever played. The point of view shifted as the eyes moved through their field of vision. There were more webbed holes and shining flecks in the distance. Martinez lost count at twelve exits when she realized those what those points of lights were. They weren't stars or crystals or bioluminescent life. They were eyeballs.

*****

"Well, we can't spear them one by one," Patel said flatly as she rehung the mirror after the scrying was finished.

"What about fire? Spider silk is really flammable," Liu suggested as she nipped off the glowing ends of the incense sticks with the fingers and stuck them upside down in the sand.

"You saw all those holes. There's no way to ensure the Harvester of Eyes wouldn't just bolt," Martinez pointed out.

"And there still isn't an exit strategy," Patel reminded them.

"We could use the compass and find which tunnel leads to the Outer Lands?" Martinez spitballed as she scrubbed down the chalk. "It seemed to work in the Magh Meall of the Upper Peninsula once we got close to the cave entrance."

"But the Outer Lands is a big place. Without an anchored circle, we have no way of knowing where in Asia we would reappear in the mortal realm," Liu conjectured as she placed the candles back in their drawer.

They mulled on the problem over another cup of tea and moved to the living room. "What if we use the rat as an exit strategy?" Martinez thought out loud.

Patel played along. "Then how would you get in? The place is covered in silk. There is no way you could approach without the demon knowing well ahead of time."

"A sending circle. We have an address, and if it works with eyeballs, why can't it work on people? If we make the circle big enough to accommodate two people, there is plenty of space to add some protections for those inside the circle and to make sure nothing comes through from the other side..." Martinez hypothesized. "I'm sure Chloe and Dot could work out the particulars for us."

"Why can't we just send a bomb through the sending circle and call Ganesha afterwards?" Liu questioned.

"I'm not sure it works that way, Hobgoblin," Patel scolded her. "Bombs—and fires, come to think of it—are messy and could do a lot of damage to the Magh Mealls connected to the lair. I'm not sure drawing a deity's attention to such a scene is a good idea."

"Light," Martinez said firmly. "You know how they always say don't look directly at the sun because it could burn your retinas and cause permanent blindness? We could burn out all those eyes with one source of light if it was sufficiently bright enough."

"And how would someone do that without also blinding themselves in the process?" Liu quizzed her.

"Magic light?" Martinez said with much less certainty.

"You know putting the word 'magic' in front of something isn't a solution," Liu goaded her.

"Except when it is," Martinez countered. "I use a lot of *magic* bullets and *magic* persuasion and *magic* detection. We just have to figure out how to *magic* light so it hurts the demon and not us."

Liu shifted in her seat. "I'm listening."

"Each time the Harvester of Eyes had been set back, it's been in the Hindu pantheon. She even avoids hunting in the subcontinent. Is there a Hindu holy light that we could harness or magic up?" Martinez asked Patel.

"Possibly," Patel reluctantly admitted, "but neither of you could do it. I would have to go in too."

Che, who had been quietly listening, spoke up for the first time. "Do you think that wise, Ms. Patel?"

The corners of her mouth lifted in an odd half-smile. "No, but the question is whether it is necessary."

"She's fully capable, and it's not like she would be going in alone," Liu reminded him.

"I have eaten more salt than you have eaten rice," Patel repeated the Cantonese idiom for her protective assistant. Liu smirked, and Martinez didn't need to know Chinese to capture the gist.

"So our plan is to esoterically mail ourselves to the Harvester of Eyes's lair, blind the eyes with sacred Hindu light, call Ganesha to keep her in her place, and use his rat to get back home," Martinez recapped.

"That sounds about right," Patel concurred.

"I've gone in with a lot less," Liu admitted.

As mission leader, Martinez called it into the Salt Mine and set the wheels in motion.

Chapter Twenty-Five

The Accursed Lair of the Harvester of Eyes
Somewhere in Time

The Harvester of Eyes was surrounded by earth, digging once more; there was little more disheartening that excavating the same corridor for a second time. She should have been suspicious when an unexpected meal walked into one of her tunnels; she was old enough to know there were no free lunches. At least she didn't have to start from her chamber; the earth elemental had stopped once it reached the edge of the middle lands. Not even a being of stone dared to enter her subterranean lair.

Her front legs shifted the loose dirt, dislodging a solid clump of dirt and rock. She carried it in her mouth and brought it back to her chamber, adding it to the growing pile. Once the passage was completely clear, she would have to move the debris again. Ironically, that repetitive work didn't bother her as much because it gave her an excuse to get out of her lair and get some fresh air. Perhaps she would treat herself to a meal afterwards; she always liked dining on exotic food.

She hadn't always been a digger, but fate had forced her

proverbial hand when she was driven underground. There was no day or night, no changes of season; nothing but the indiscernible passage of time—and she had lived an eternity. She'd kept waiting for her wounds to heal and her sight to return, but it never did. For the longest time, she only had just the one tunnel for feeding. She'd skulked in the shadows and ambushed prey, evading the fae who despised her kind. And then she'd found a new way of seeing. Suddenly, the tunnel held more promise, and she enthusiastically built more.

Once she could enter the mortal realm, each one opened a new world to her and expanded her sight. She voyeuristically watched all of creation unfold through mortal eyes. Each individual eye was myopic in vision—skewed and colored by culture and personal experience—but when aggregated, a much larger picture came into focus. It gave the mortal realm texture and depth. The more she saw, the more she wanted to see, and she harvested progressively greater number of eyes to quench her insatiable curiosity. In hindsight, she was willing to admit that she might have gone overboard at first, but who could blame a thirsty creature for drinking deep at the well?

Devas, that's who! She spat out the thought like a bad taste in her mouth. She'd tried to live within their confines, but as the world changed faster and more abruptly, it was impossible to keep up with all the variation and progress. She discovered new continents from one visit to the next. Entire kingdoms were wiped out before she could make a return visit. Old religions begat new ones as they found greater specificity and points of division.

Worse was having a dud in the mix when she'd waited so long to reap her precious forty-nine eyes. The narrow collection time made it impossible for her to travel everywhere and severely hampered her ability to cherry pick whose eyes she took. Fortunately, she didn't have to worry about that anymore.

Using rakshasas to gather more eyes on her behalf meant she could have a constant supply streaming in from everywhere except Asia, which she could hunt herself. The failure of Popo's pack was regrettable, but only a minor setback because the endeavor was a positive proof of concept. Now she knew that rakshasas could enter the mortal realm as long as she got them to a middle land outside of Asia. The sending circle worked, as evidenced by the few eyes they did manage to send before being banished. And more importantly, she now had insight into a whole new part of the mortal realm: the Upper Peninsula, whatever that was. It was only a matter of time before the operation could go large scale, and she had nothing but time.

As she worked on the next chunk, she perceived a tremor somewhere in her extensive web. She ceased her labor and used her mental map to follow the vibration back to its source; it was coming from her lair. *Was it possible one of Popo's pack had eluded ambush and continues to send eyes?* she pondered. *That would be a rakshasi worthy of leading her own troop.* She bit another hunk of rock and carried it back through the tunnel—

the key to excavation was to never waste a trip.

*****

Martinez, Liu, and Patel appeared in the middle of the cavern surrounded by a myriad of eyeballs. It was a bumpier ride than entering the Magh Meall, but not nearly as bad as Korean shaman travel. If this was anything like what summoned creatures had to go through when they were called to the mortal realm, it was little wonder why they were so cranky upon arrival.

Martinez and Liu did a visual sweep with their weapons drawn, and once they cleared the area, they got to work. Martinez had brought her night vision goggles, but the gleaming eyeballs created enough light to operate. Without lids, they could not blink and the phenomenon was most unnerving. The orbs tracked the movement reflexively, and the trio worked quickly, unaware if the demon could see them through the eyes and how much time they had before she would be upon them.

Martinez pulled out the compass that still contained a piece of the rakshasi's tail and rotated in place until the needle pointed true. She gave a hand signal to Liu, who unsheathed a dagger and strategically cut a path to the hole while disturbing as few silk threads as possible. The Outer Lands was their backup exit strategy in case things went badly.

Martinez kept watch with her Glock while Patel unfurled

her will and focused it into her mantra: *Om Namah Shivaya*. It roughly translated to "adoration to Lord Shiva," one the deities in the Hindu trinity, along with Brahma and Vishnu. Shiva was one of the supreme beings who creates, protects, and transforms the universe, and his moniker as the Destroyer was better understood in opposition to Vishnu the Preserver. Transformation was a destructive process, and sometimes you had to raze a site in order to build something better.

The words themselves held great symbolic power to Hindus. *Om* was the vibration of the universe, the sympathetic resonance of the soul. The five-syllable mantra evoked universal consciousness as a singularity, each representing one of the five elements: earth, water, fire, air, and ether. When spoken by a magician who subtextually understood such things, the effects could be paradigm-shifting, which was exactly what Patel wanted. As she repeated the words in her mind, she rolled the energy into itself, compounding the magic.

Her insides warmed, and it felt like every molecule of her being was ricocheting inside her consciousness. Martinez could feel the heat coming off her, and she donned her sunglasses and whistled for Liu to do the same. It was about to get real bright.

When Patel could no longer contain the pent-up light within her, she spoke the mantra aloud with authority, "*Om Namah Shivaya!*" She lit up like a supernova, and the holy light escaped through every pore of her skin. It cut through clothing, webs, and stone; nothing could hide from its righteous splendor. The eyeballs couldn't stop themselves for gazing on her radiance. Even when it hurt, they couldn't turn away. They looked until they wept. They stared until they bled.

A horrendous shriek echoed through the cavern. Martinez and Liu took defensive stances, but it was impossible to tell which hole the sound was coming from. All they knew was that something big was coming in fast.

"I think it worked. Time to call the big guy," Martinez yelled over the reverberations. Patel waited for most of the light to leave her body before redirecting her will to a different mantra: *Om Gam Ganapataye Namah*.

Their first sight of the Harvester of Eyes was breathtaking. She was ten feet tall and just as long. Her black lustrous shell gleamed in the receding light, and her eight crimson legs skittered in a coordinated fashion. The wounds Varaha had given her still seeped serous fluid, and her mouth was oversized with fangs that hinged in a downward stab. *I was blind long before this*, the demon broadcast telepathically. *That will not stop me from rending you in two!*

Patel ran down the path cleared by Liu while Martinez provided cover, aiming for the demon's fleshy parts around the face and mouth. The banishment magic in the bullets wouldn't work—the Harvester of Eyes was already home—but she hoped they would help keep the demon off them until Ganesha showed up. She unloaded a magazine into the primordial spider, who flinched with each hit but continued her charge. She saw

Liu circle behind the monstrous beast and quickly changed to a fresh magazine as she hustled behind Patel. They were rapidly running out of cavern.

With lightning speed, Liu bisected the demon's path perpendicularly and slid underneath her and slashed along the gap in the spider's exoskeleton used for spinning silk. The Harvester of Eyes halted her advance and wailed in pain.

Martinez raised her Glock for another salvo of fire when a lasso appeared out of thin air and landed around the Harvester of Eyes's neck. Martinez followed the rope to the other end and saw Ganesha, one-tusked elephant head and all. Her brain railed against the power of his presence, blue and four armed. Instead of ceremonial regalia, he was majestically girded for battle. He tightened the noose around the demon and she writhed. The fibers burned despite her hardened armor.

"Netra zasyacchid, you have exceeded your bounds. Can you not restrain your mischief?" he asked her rhetorically.

"Who are you to censure me?" she hissed and howled.

He trumpeted loudly and declared, "I am Lord Vinayagar, son of Shiva, Lord of Hosts. Your deeds have been seen. May you choose more wisely in the future."

Liu sprinted away from the deva and demon to join Martinez and Patel at the exit that led to the Outer Lands. She sliced through the web and suggested a hasty retreat. "Come on, I think he's got it from here."

As they entered the dark passage, Martinez broke a glow

stick and shook the contents. The soft green light was enough for them to keep their footing on the uneven terrain, even as the ground periodically shook behind them. Eventually the fetid air started to clear, and there was a moist warmth ahead.

The tunnel opened into a cave with a bubbling pool, a hot spring judging by the ambient temperature of the room. Patel leaned heavily against the wall; the casting had taken its toll. Martinez handed her the grounded canteen while Liu kept watch on the entrances: they were in rakshasa territory now.

A great rumble and cloud of dust came out of the passage behind them. A giant boulder appeared, branded with an eight-spoke wheel, sealing the way. It was one of the oldest and most enduring symbols in Indus Valley civilizations, evoking the wheel of law in Sanskrit as well as Buddha's first teaching and universal moral order. Stamping that on the sealed exit was a serious metaphysical ward.

"Remind me never to piss off Ganesha," Liu reacted at the sight of the *dhammachakra* and shifted her focus to the lone exit leading out of the cave while Martinez and Liu set up shop to summon a rat.

It didn't seem any safer in the Outer Lands at large, so it was quickly decided to remain in the cave and hope the threat of the Harvester of Eyes was enough to keep most wandering creatures away. They put their backs against the wall and pulled out the prasad. None of them knew exactly how this worked, but Liu insisted on tying Ariadne's string to the satchel, just in case the rat tried to run off with it. Patel wrapped the other end of the string around her finger a few times, and they caught their breath as the adrenaline wore off.

"That was impressive," Martinez said to Patel. "Have you always been able to do that?"

Patel gave her a genuine smile. "In Tamil, Kanali means the sun."

"And that's why Leader calls you Prism," Martinez put two and two together.

"Perhaps, but I try not to retro-engineer Leader's process. It only leads to headaches," the Indian woman gently advised. "How's your first year going?"

Martinez did a quick tally. "Well, this is not my first demon. Or my first contact to another plane besides the Magh Meall. But it was my first deity and definitely the first time I've been waiting for a rodent to catch a ride home."

"You're not being entirely truthful," Liu said, "Stigma's been crashing at your place for months now."

"He's alive?" Patel cooed with a tilt of her head. "Good, I always liked him." She felt a tug at the string and saw a rat appear in the space between her and Liu. He held the bottom of the satchel in his mouth and yanked on it as he walked backward.

"Greetings, Kraunsha." Patel bowed her head to him, and the rat released the bag and stood up on his hind legs in recognition of her polite address. "I bid you to take the three of us back to the mortal realm to my home in Melaka City. This is but a small token of our appreciation. I have an entire box of laddus waiting for you when we arrive."

Patel careful opened the sack and present the rat with the prasad. He placed his small front paws on the edge of her palm and ate the heavenly sweet out of her right hand. When he was certain he'd licked any remaining syrup, he dropped down on the ground and grew in size.

They grabbed their gear and climbed on top of the rat's back. It squeaked a little as Liu's knees dug in. "What?" she said defensively. "I don't want to fall off." The rat's long tail wrapped around their collective midsections, and Liu eased her grip. With his passengers secured, Kraunsha walked through the wall of rock and into the sunny meditation room in Patel's Malaysian estate where Che was nervously pacing.

The rat unwound its tail and the women slid off his back. Che was unfazed by the rodent of unusual size, but he was so relieved to see Patel, he almost smiled. Kraunsha shrank back to reasonable size and squeaked again.

Patel tucked a stray hair behind her ear and nodded. "Of course. Mukarto, could you retrieve the box of laddus in the kitchen for our honored guest?"

Epilogue

Joan Liu put the minced garlic in a small dish next to the diced onion, carrot, and celery for the dressing to be cooked by Allison. Liu looked down her to-do list and her next assignment was assembling the crudités platter. Their relationship was predicated on each person playing to their strengths, and while Liu wasn't a very good cook, she could handle cutting raw vegetables for dip.

She cleaned off the board so everything didn't taste like garlic and onions, and Claire came running by at top speed. Allison looked up from her latest round of basting with a stern frown.

"Claire, what did I say about running in the kitchen?! There are a lot of hot pots and pans and knives."

"Sorry, mommy!" she called out on the way to the backyard.

Allison closed the oven door and took a deep breath in and out. "I love that child more than life itself. I'm not going to wring her neck."

Liu smirked. "She's five—"

"She's four and a half," Allison corrected her. Clair drove her crazy at times, but she wouldn't give away six months with her so lightly.

"She's four and a half," Liu restarted. "That's what four and a half year olds do."

"Says the woman with no children," Allison retorted as she washed her hands and pulled the kitchen towel off the bowl. The dome of the risen dough was round and full, and Allison deflated it with a satisfying punch to the center. She dusted the board and her hands with flour and started shaping the dinner rolls for a second proof.

Liu knew the signs of a potential fight better than anyone and kept her head down. She pulled out the platter and made quick work of the celery and carrot sticks before slicing the cauliflower into bite-size florets with handles for dipping. "You know we could cater this next year. Or maybe make it a potluck? I'm sure there are plenty of LBGTQ people who would love to whip out their mother's deviled egg recipe or try that casserole they saw on food network. We could give the young ones mashed potatoes. Even *I* can make mashed potatoes."

Her self-deprecation elicited a smile from Allison, which lifted the mood. "It will be fine once everyone gets here," she asserted. "The holidays are just hard."

Liu secured the knife under the board and gave her a big hug from behind. "I know. We don't have say in who our biologic families are, but we always have a choice in the company we keep and the life we build with them."

Allison stifled her tears as she heard Claire open the door. The little girl ran inside but slowed down as she entered the kitchen. Allison smiled—it was a rare and precious thing to have definitive proof that your child was listening to you. Her cheeks were flush and the light sweat on her brow suggested it was more from the exertion than the cold. "Mommy, can I have something to drink?" she piped up.

Liu stepped in as Allison was knuckle deep in dough and her hands were covered in flour. "I've got this. You keep rolling those balls," she announced mischievously and gave Allison a kiss on the shoulder. Liu opened the fridge; it resembled a game of Tetris or possibly a Jenga tower. She managed to grab a juice box without everything falling apart and handed it to Claire.

Liu watched the little girl free the straw and stab the hole with the delight kids take in doing a thing right. She drained half of it without pausing to breathe and smacked her lips when she was done. "Better?" Liu asked her.

"Yes. Thank you," Claire politely replied and handed Liu the empty container and wrapper.

Her mother tutted, "Claire, Joan is not your slave. You know where the trash can is." Liu held out her hand and gave Claire the opportunity for a do-over. The serious girl nodded and threw her own trash away.

Liu patted her back. "Come on, kiddo, let's go outside and give mommy a moment."

Claire looked up confused. "Don't you have to help?"

"Oh, believe me, I'm helping," she said with just a hint of sarcasm. "Last one to the slide is a rotten egg!"

Claire perked up and fast-walked to the edge of the kitchen before taking off at the full sprint. "Hey, no fair! I didn't say 'go'!" Liu called out. Allison mouthed *thank you* as Liu gave faux chase, letting Claire win by a hair.

Liu was small and light enough to play in Claire's backyard set, and after a few creative variations of tag, she managed to tire out the energetic girl without exhausting herself in the process. When she re-entered the house with Claire on one hip, snoring softly, Allison had managed to get the rest of the prep work done, and the pans were lined up in order of their slot in the coveted oven rotation.

Liu carried Claire to her room and put her to bed for a nap. It was going to be a long night with lots of "boring grown-up stuff"; Christmas was for kids, Thanksgiving for adults. A glass of wine was waiting for her at the kitchen table in one of the few spots not dedicated to food staging. "You're a life saver," Allison spoke tenderly and squeezed Liu's hand. "I couldn't have pulled it off without you."

Liu smiled and took a seat. "That's what girlfriends are for." She tipped the glass back and gave her approval on the bottle.

Liu's phone buzzed in her pocket and Allison's face froze.

"Is it work?" she asked.

Liu shook her head. "No, just Teresa wishing us a happy Thanksgiving," she replied and flipped the phone around. The picture centered on a tall metal pot on a propane-fueled burner sitting on a platform of cinderblocks. A hooked turkey dangled above the pot from a tripod contraption. Not far from the rig was a very large fire extinguisher. *Just in case. Happy Turkey Day.*

*****

Wilson rang the doorbell of his Corktown House, and within, the Westminster clock chimed. He was never one for celebrating Thanksgiving in the traditional sense, but he couldn't remember the last time he was actually invited to such a dinner and decided to come. He was still on leave and hadn't seen Martinez or Haddock since his return from Avalon, and he was suddenly very self-conscious of how big his winter jacket had become in his lean state.

Martinez opened the door and greeted him with a big smile. "Wilson, come in!" It felt a little weird being invited into his own house, but the wards were hers now, even if he'd been the one who first inscribed the sigils. Martinez closed the door and hung his coat in the closet. "And this must be kitty?" She pointed to the cat carrier he held in one hand.

"Yes. I just got her and I didn't want to leave her at home

by herself," Wilson explained as he opened the cage door. Mau slinked out and assessed her new surroundings. Wilson had expected more pushback from Mau on using the carrier, but much to his surprise, she put up no protest. It made sense for humans to carry cats in special palanquins, although she didn't care for the modern aesthetic.

"Isn't she a pretty thing?" Martinez cooed and held out her hand to let Mau sniff her. "Are you hungry?"

Mau did not answer; Wilson had already explained that sometimes humans talk to cats like they can talk back, but normal cats *definitely* do not answer out loud. Instead, she purred and rubbed up against Martinez's hand. Martinez petted her velvety coat, which had grown thick with the cold weather. "Let's go to the kitchen and see if we can find you something."

The table was covered by an embroidered tablecloth and each place setting was topped with a linen napkin folded into a crown. A quick count informed Wilson he was not the only one coming to dinner.

"Where's Aaron?" Wilson asked.

"Watching the bird. Twelve pounds of turkey cooked to perfection in forty-five minutes in the fryer," Martinez answered triumphantly. She placed a dish of cooked gizzards and organ meat she'd used to make the gravy on the kitchen floor. "There you go, kitty. Eat up." Mau approached the dish and ate with relish. The Mountain had given her the prized organs: heart, liver, lungs—all the things placed in sacred canopic jars.

"Do you want to try his signature beverage?" Martinez asked with a trace of sarcasm.

Wilson smirked and suddenly looked very familiar despite his thinness. "Sure."

She poured a pale red elixir into a cup and asked over her shoulder, "Alcohol or seltzer water?"

Wilson shrugged. "I'm not driving anytime soon."

"Prosecco it is," she cheered as she poured the bubbly.

The sliding door to the backyard opened, and Haddock's voice entered before him. "Bird's ready, fire's off, the pot is covered, and as long as I don't do anything stupid, like pour the boiling hot oil on dried leaves, we shouldn't need the fire extinguisher."

They saw the bird first: golden brown, crispy skin and still cracking from the fryer. Haddock did not look so majestic, covered with a full apron, long gloves, and a ridiculous-looking plastic face shield that looked like surplus chemistry equipment. "This may be the coolest thing I've ever done," he declared.

The smell was amazing, and Mau looked up in interest. She had finished licking the last of the gravy from her dish and was ready for seconds. She meowed.

"You made it!" Haddock gestured with his head to Wilson. "And you must be the new kitty," he addressed the cat sitting regally on its haunches. "It's too hot to eat now, but see me later tonight." Haddock winked conspiratorially. On first pass, both the Mountain and the Jester were all right in Mau's esteem.

"Do you guys need any help?" Wilson offered.

"Nope. Everything that needs to be in the oven is just cooking through, we'll cut the bird once it rests, and the pies are already baked but we'll warm them up while we eat." Martinez replied as she cleared a space on the counter for the turkey.

"Kitty!" A high-pitched squeal from thin air caught them all by surprise. They were all familiar with the Quaker ghosts that lived in the house, but it was first time any of them had heard the little girl speak.

Millie's transparent figure emerged from the wall, chastising the child. "Come back here. You know they are having a party tonight—oh, Mr. Wilson! It's been so long. My, you look so thin." Martinez snickered behind her cup—only Millie could say what they were all thinking.

"I was away for a long time, and they didn't have very good food there," Wilson explained simply.

"Well, I daresay that won't be a problem tonight!" Millie exclaimed. "They've been planning and cooking up a storm."

The quiet one pulled a ribbon out of her hair and ran circles around Mau, who instinctually batted at the end with her paw. She knew she could catch the Powerful One's ribbon if she was on the same plane of existence. Mau looked up to Wilson. *I can play?*

Wilson sighed. *Only because they are friends, but normally, it's not a good idea.*

Mau grinned and phased out of substantial form,

surprising Martinez and Haddock. Once she was diaphanous, she pounced with both front paws and caught the ribbon. She smugly flicked her tail. The girl squealed with delight and petted Mau with abandon. "Gentle," Millie cautioned her, which struck Martinez as patently ridiculous, yet incredibly endearing. There was no way to pet a cat too hard when their body was insubstantial, but Millie's empathy persisted into death.

"Why don't you play with kitty upstairs and when she gets hungry, she can come down," Martinez suggested. The quiet one disappeared into the wall and Mau chased after her.

"What a Thanksgiving treat!" Millie declared before following the pair.

Martinez and Haddock knew better than to ask questions, and they proceeded with dinner preparations as if they hadn't just seen a cat turn into a ghost cat, but eventually Wilson felt silly saying nothing, so he gave Martinez a friendly a heads-up. "You may want to stock up on tuna, in case she gets hungry when she's visiting."

"I'll add it to the grocery list," she said breezily.

"David, what do think of the cranberry milk punch?" Haddock changed the topic.

"It's nice—spiced, smooth and tart, but not too sweet," he replied nonchalantly.

Haddock didn't bother to hide his surprise. "Since when did you get a taste palate?"

"Everything tastes better when you're as thin as I am," he joked darkly.

"Well, I have amuse bouche to fix that," Martinez replied and pulled out trays and platters of bite-sized nibbles. "Let's move this to the living room. LaSalle should be arriving any minute with the rest of the crew." Haddock shed his protective gear and followed her lead with the drink station in hand.

"Leader's coming?" Wilson balked.

"No, she sent her regards and a nice bottle of wine. But LaSalle is giving Harold, Chloe, and Dot a ride," Martinez answered as she set up the hors d'oeuvres. Haddock started his dinner party playlist and it started out with some mellow instrumentals.

Wilson loaded his plate with a sampling. "I don't think I've ever seen LaSalle without Leader nearby," he puzzled.

Martinez shrugged and popped an olive into her mouth. "I invited her but she said she had other plans."

Haddock dramatically raised the question and his right eyebrow. "Makes you wonder what Leader's thankful for this year?"

THE END

The agents of The Salt Mine will return in *Brain Drain*

Printed in Great Britain
by Amazon

67217736R00139